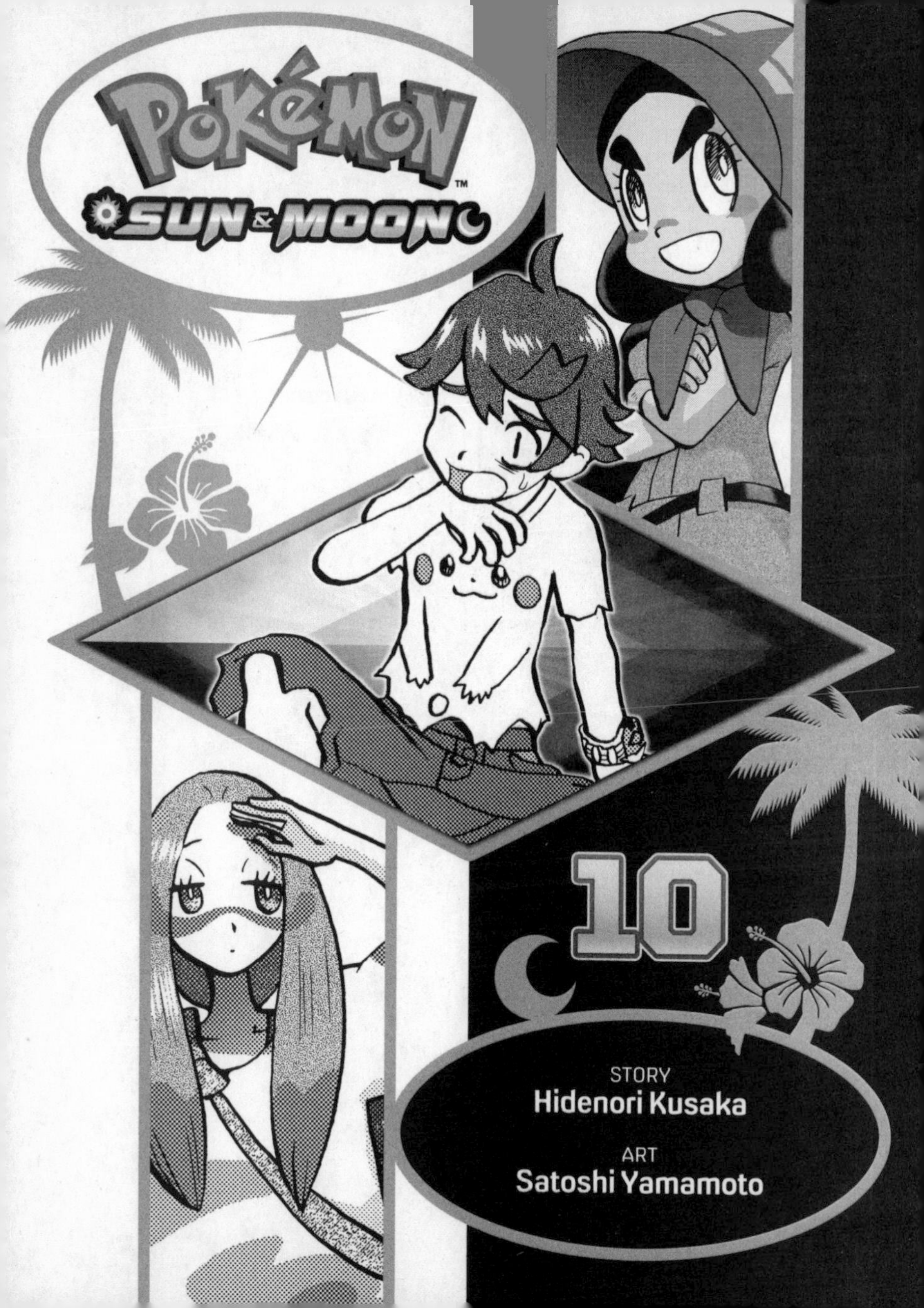

Pokémon™ Sun & Moon

10

STORY
Hidenori Kusaka

ART
Satoshi Yamamoto

Introduction

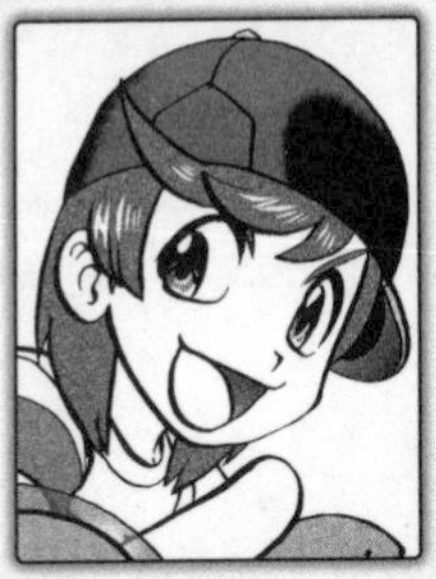

Sun

A cheerful delivery boy who paid Faba one million dollars, was betrayed by him and then got sucked into a crack in the sky. Now he's missing!

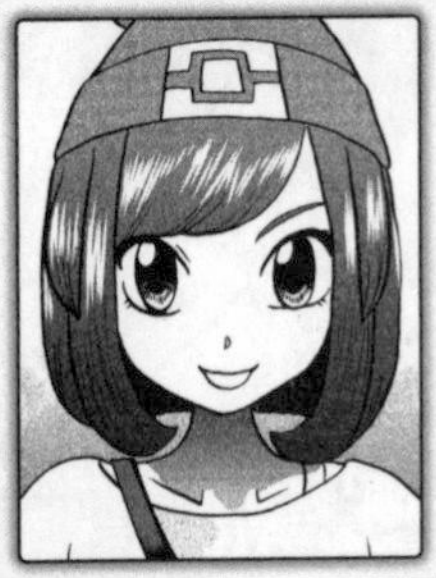

Moon

A pharmacist who has traveled to Alola from a faraway region. She is a self-confident, original thinker and an excellent archer.

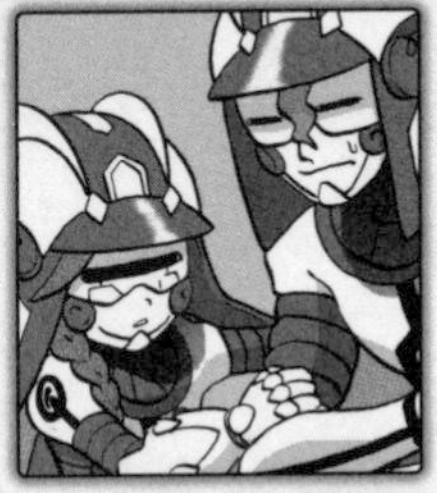

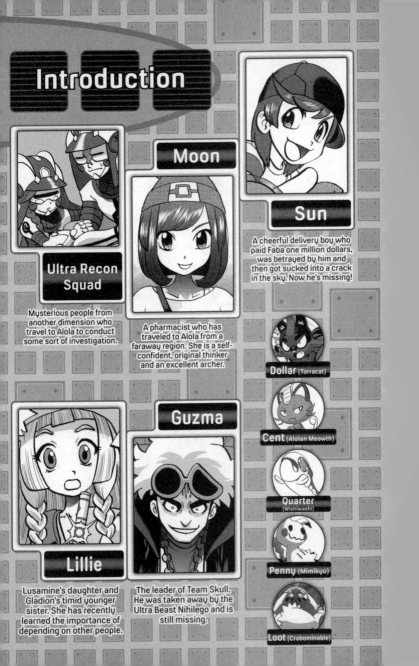

Ultra Recon Squad

Mysterious people from another dimension who travel to Alola to conduct some sort of investigation.

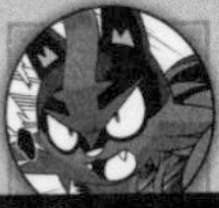

Dollar (Torracat)

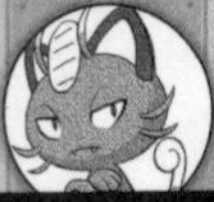

Cent (Alolan Meowth)

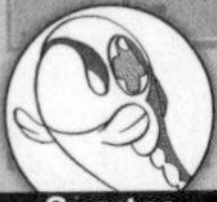

Quarter (Wishiwashi)

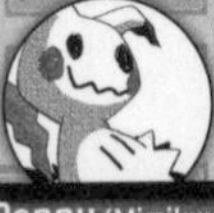

Penny (Mimikyu)

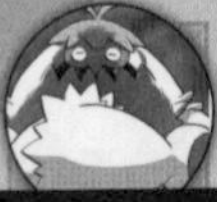

Loot (Crabominable)

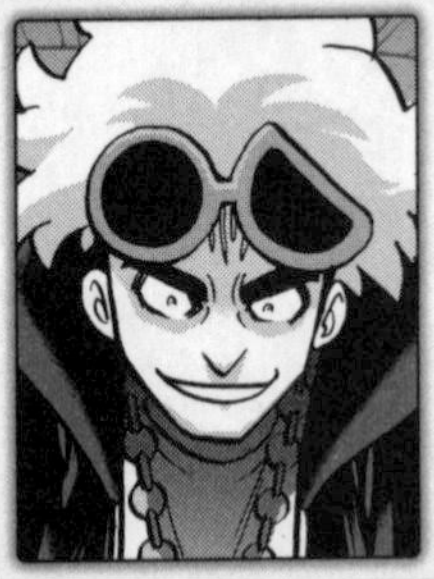

Guzma

The leader of Team Skull. He was taken away by the Ultra Beast Nihilego and is still missing.

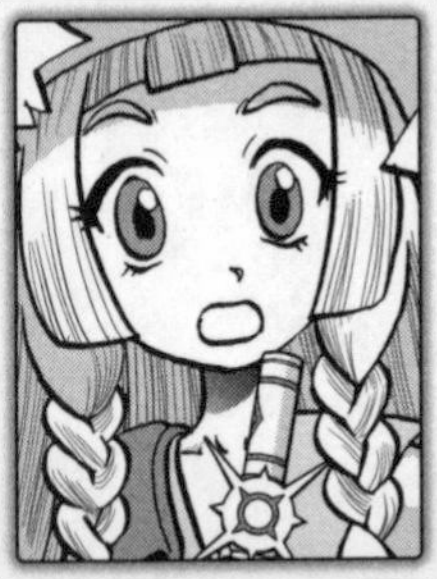

Lillie

Lusamine's daughter and Gladion's timid younger sister. She has recently learned the importance of depending on other people.

Character

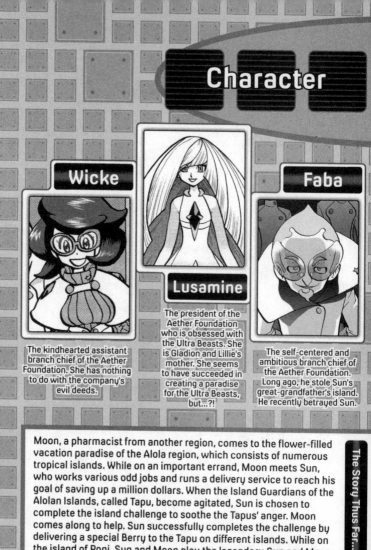

Wicke

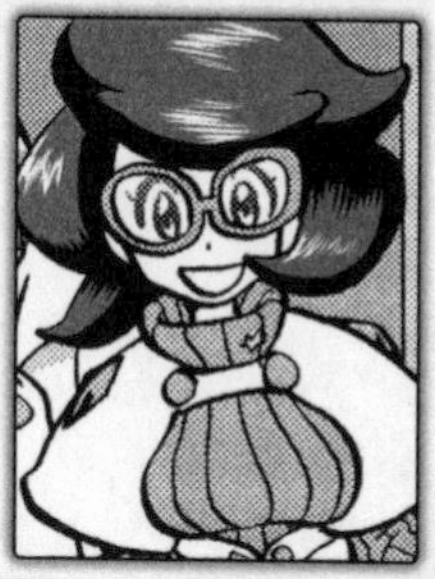

The kindhearted assistant branch chief of the Aether Foundation. She has nothing to do with the company's evil deeds.

Lusamine

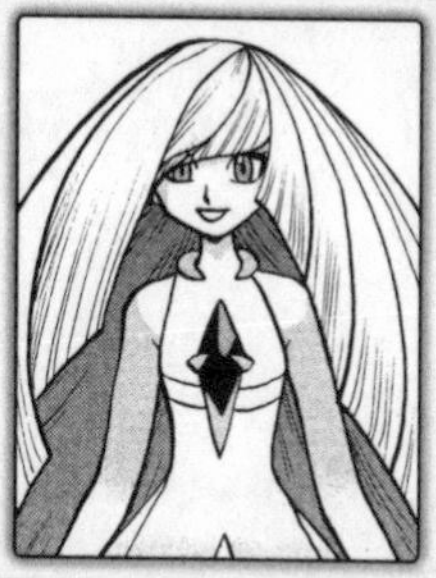

The president of the Aether Foundation who is obsessed with the Ultra Beasts. She is Gladion and Lillie's mother. She seems to have succeeded in creating a paradise for the Ultra Beasts, but...?!

Faba

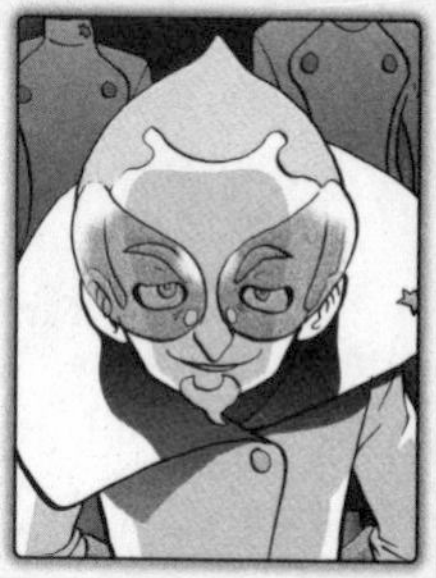

The self-centered and ambitious branch chief of the Aether Foundation. Long ago, he stole Sun's great-grandfather's island. He recently betrayed Sun.

The Story Thus Far...

Moon, a pharmacist from another region, comes to the flower-filled vacation paradise of the Alola region, which consists of numerous tropical islands. While on an important errand, Moon meets Sun, who works various odd jobs and runs a delivery service to reach his goal of saving up a million dollars. When the Island Guardians of the Alolan Islands, called Tapu, become agitated, Sun is chosen to complete the island challenge to soothe the Tapus' anger. Moon comes along to help. Sun successfully completes the challenge by delivering a special Berry to the Tapu on different islands. While on the island of Poni, Sun and Moon play the legendary Sun and Moon flutes, causing two Cosmoem to transform into Solgaleo, the emissary of the sun, and Lunala, the emissary of the moon! Then a black claw reaches out from a crack in the sky and drags Sun through the crack! Moon quickly chases after him, but where have they gone?!

CONTENTS

Zzt zzt... ♪

Adventure 29
Darkness!! The Mysterious Claws of Necrozma!

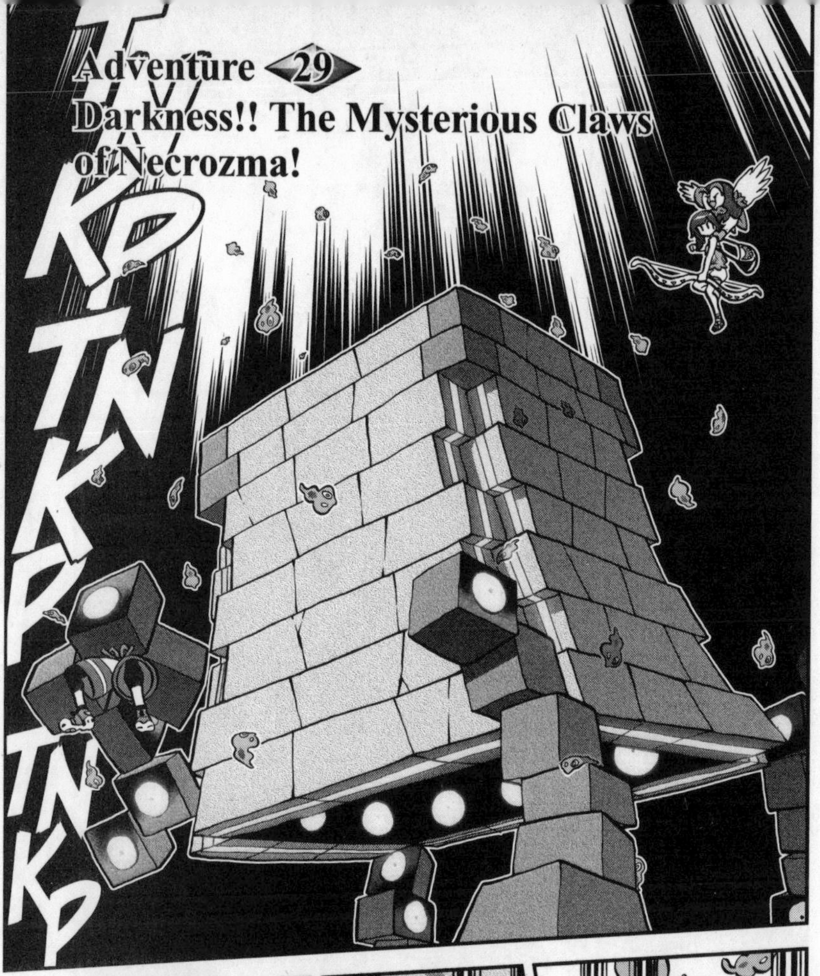
KP TNKP TNKP

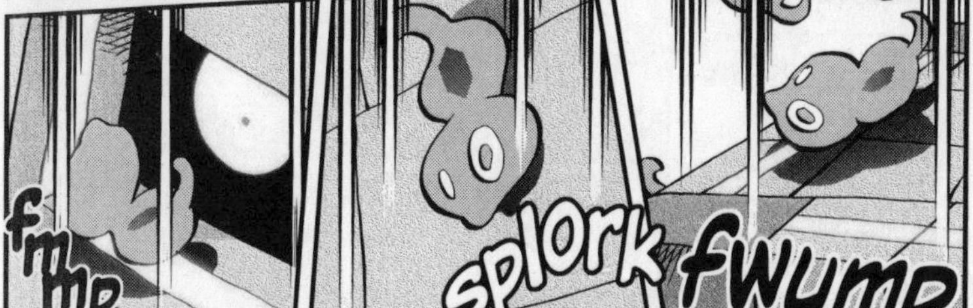
fwump
splork
frmp

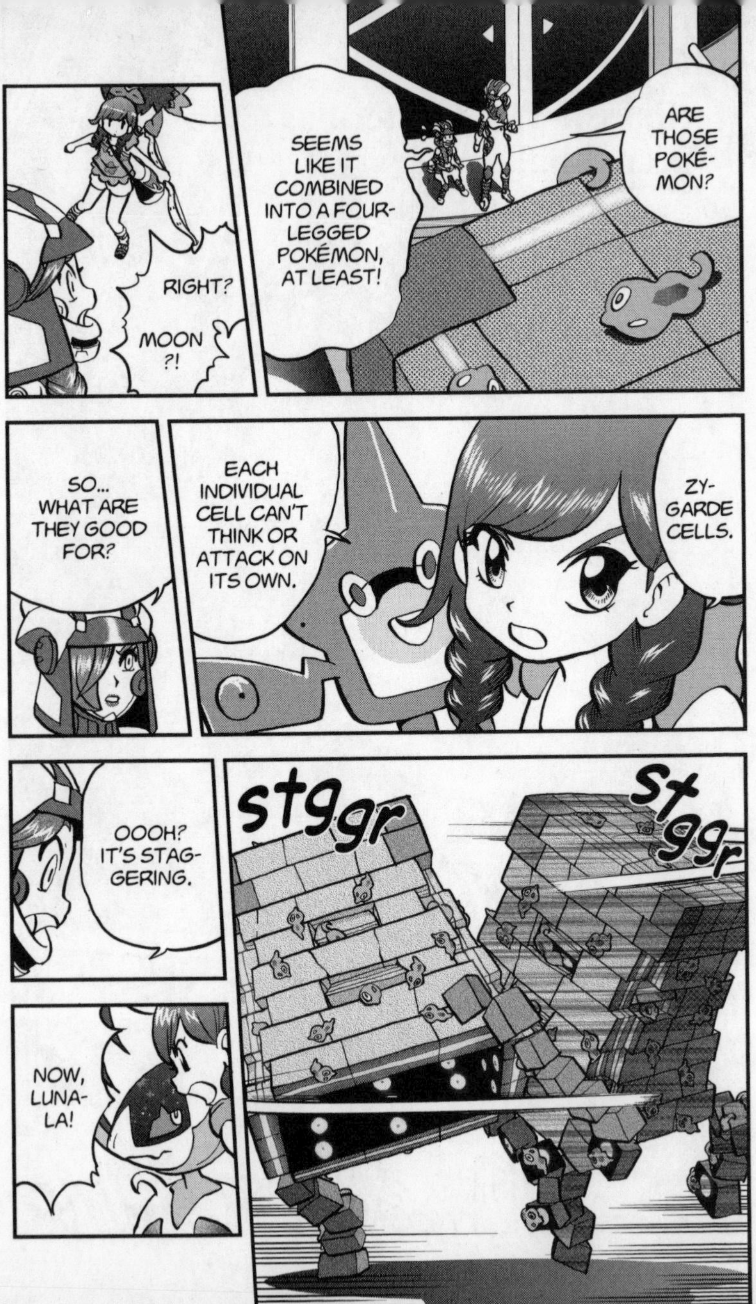
ARE THOSE POKÉMON?
SEEMS LIKE IT COMBINED INTO A FOUR-LEGGED POKÉMON, AT LEAST!
RIGHT?
MOON ?!
ZY-GARDE CELLS.
EACH INDIVIDUAL CELL CAN'T THINK OR ATTACK ON ITS OWN.
SO... WHAT ARE THEY GOOD FOR?
stggr
stggr
OOOH? IT'S STAG-GERING.
NOW, LUNA-LA!

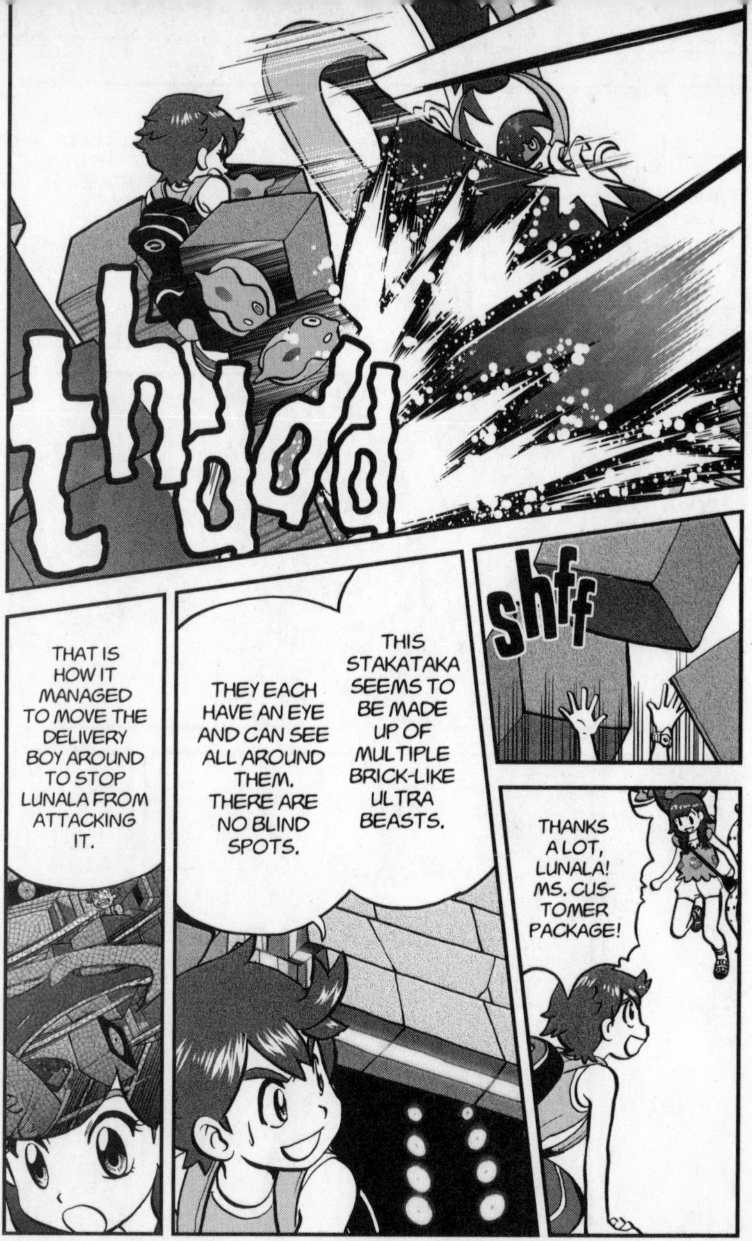
thudd
shff
THANKS A LOT, LUNALA! MS. CUSTOMER PACKAGE!
THIS STAKATAKA SEEMS TO BE MADE UP OF MULTIPLE BRICK-LIKE ULTRA BEASTS.
THEY EACH HAVE AN EYE AND CAN SEE ALL AROUND THEM. THERE ARE NO BLIND SPOTS.
THAT IS HOW IT MANAGED TO MOVE THE DELIVERY BOY AROUND TO STOP LUNALA FROM ATTACKING IT.

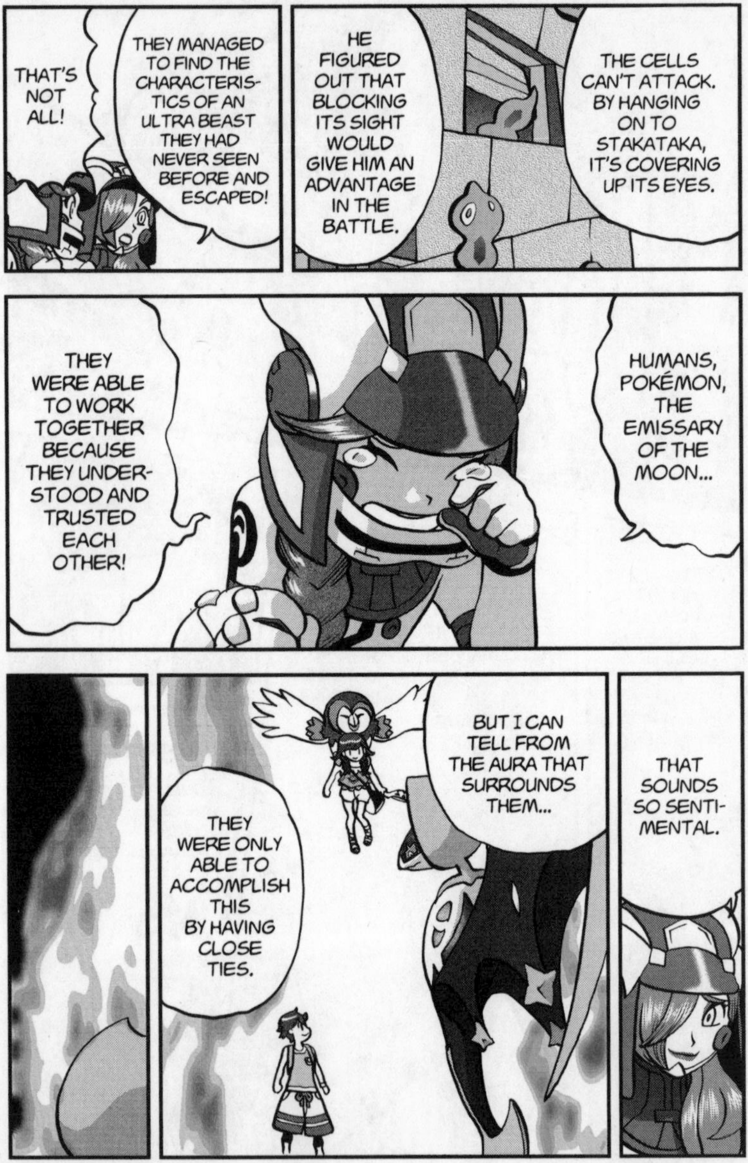
THE CELLS CAN'T ATTACK. BY HANGING ON TO STAKATAKA, IT'S COVERING UP ITS EYES.
HE FIGURED OUT THAT BLOCKING ITS SIGHT WOULD GIVE HIM AN ADVANTAGE IN THE BATTLE.
THEY MANAGED TO FIND THE CHARACTERISTICS OF AN ULTRA BEAST THEY HAD NEVER SEEN BEFORE AND ESCAPED!
THAT'S NOT ALL!
HUMANS, POKÉMON, THE EMISSARY OF THE MOON...
THEY WERE ABLE TO WORK TOGETHER BECAUSE THEY UNDERSTOOD AND TRUSTED EACH OTHER!
THAT SOUNDS SO SENTIMENTAL.
BUT I CAN TELL FROM THE AURA THAT SURROUNDS THEM...
THEY WERE ONLY ABLE TO ACCOMPLISH THIS BY HAVING CLOSE TIES.

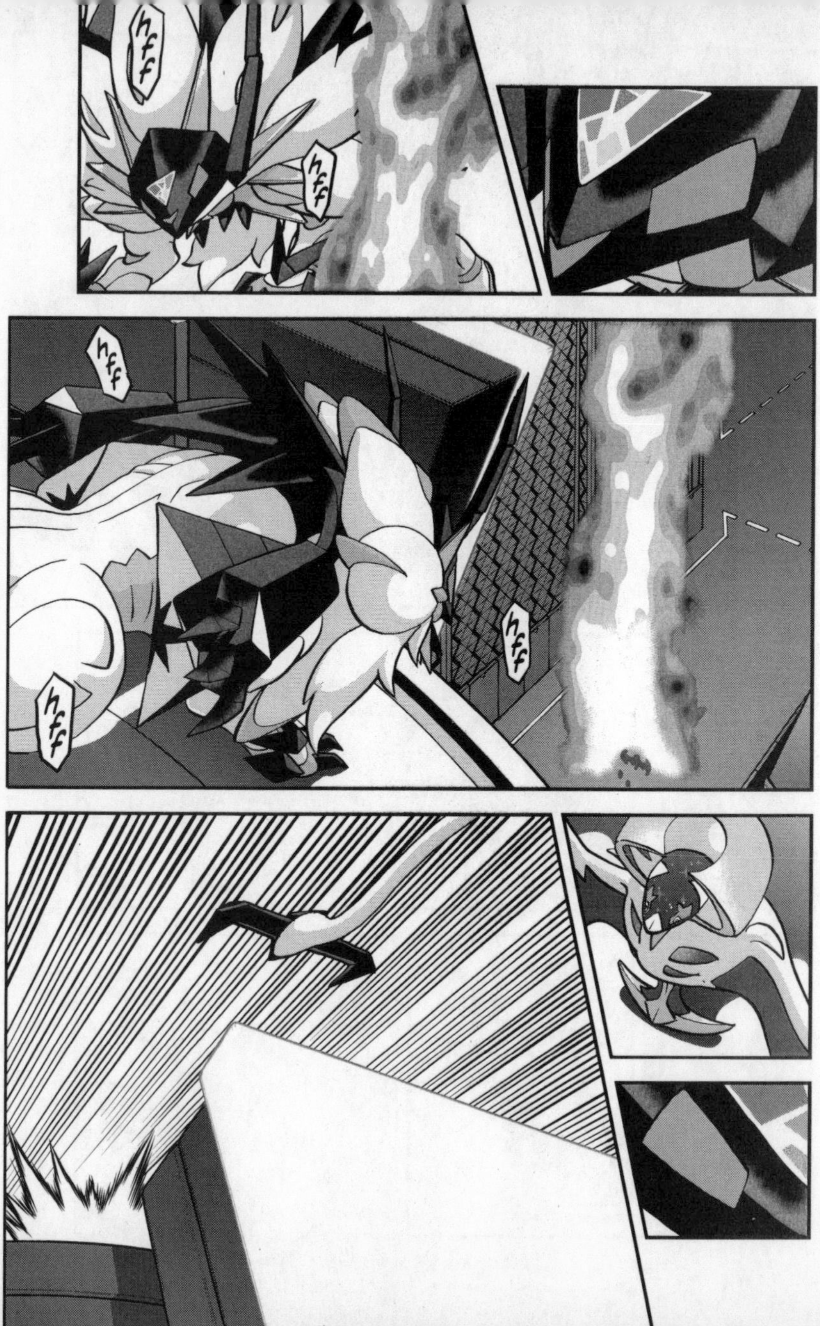
hff
hff
hff
hff
hff

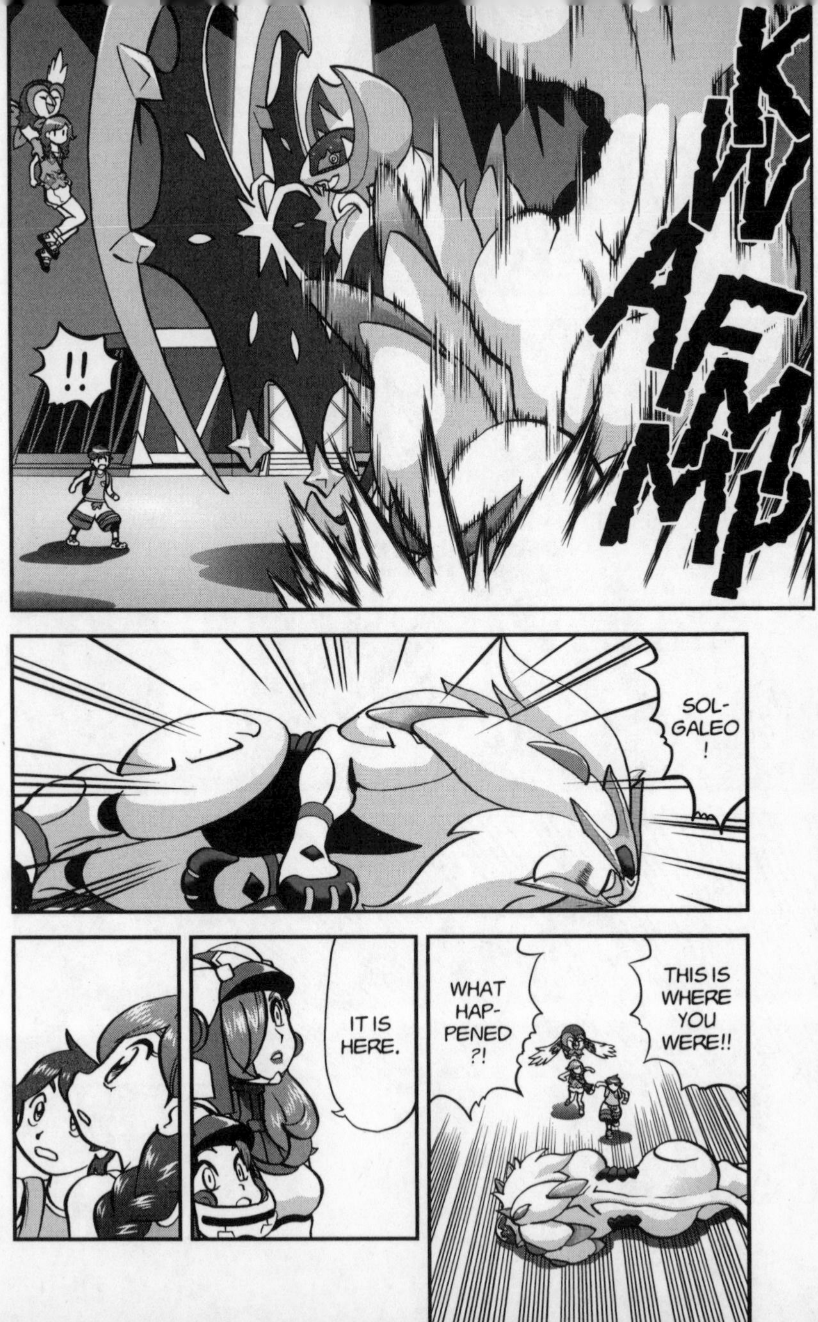
KWAFMMP
!!
SOL-GALEO!
THIS IS WHERE YOU WERE!!
WHAT HAP-PENED?!
IT IS HERE.

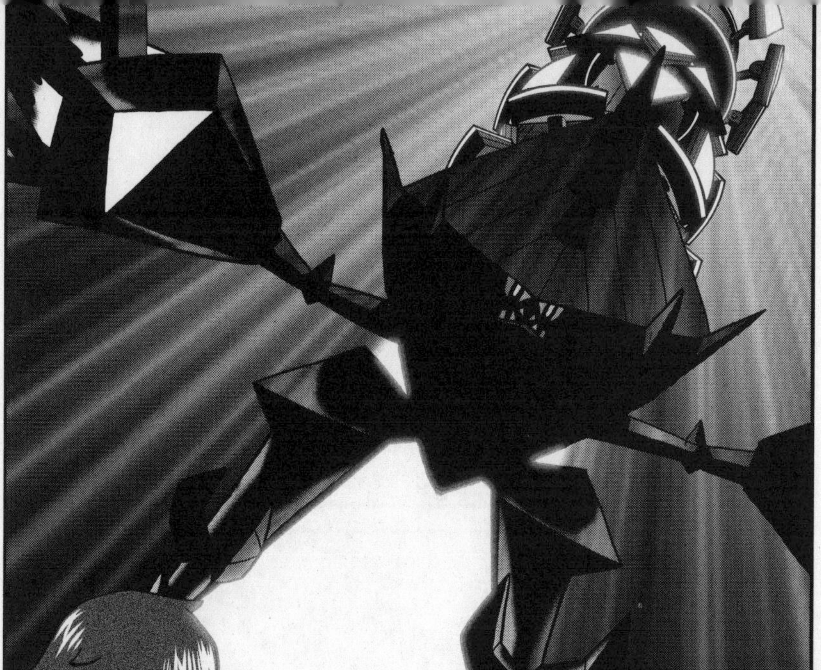

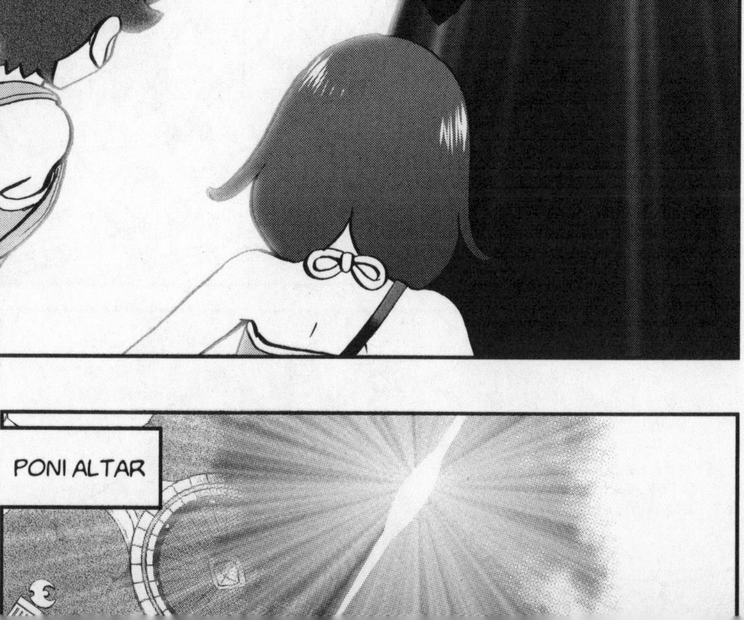
PONI ALTAR

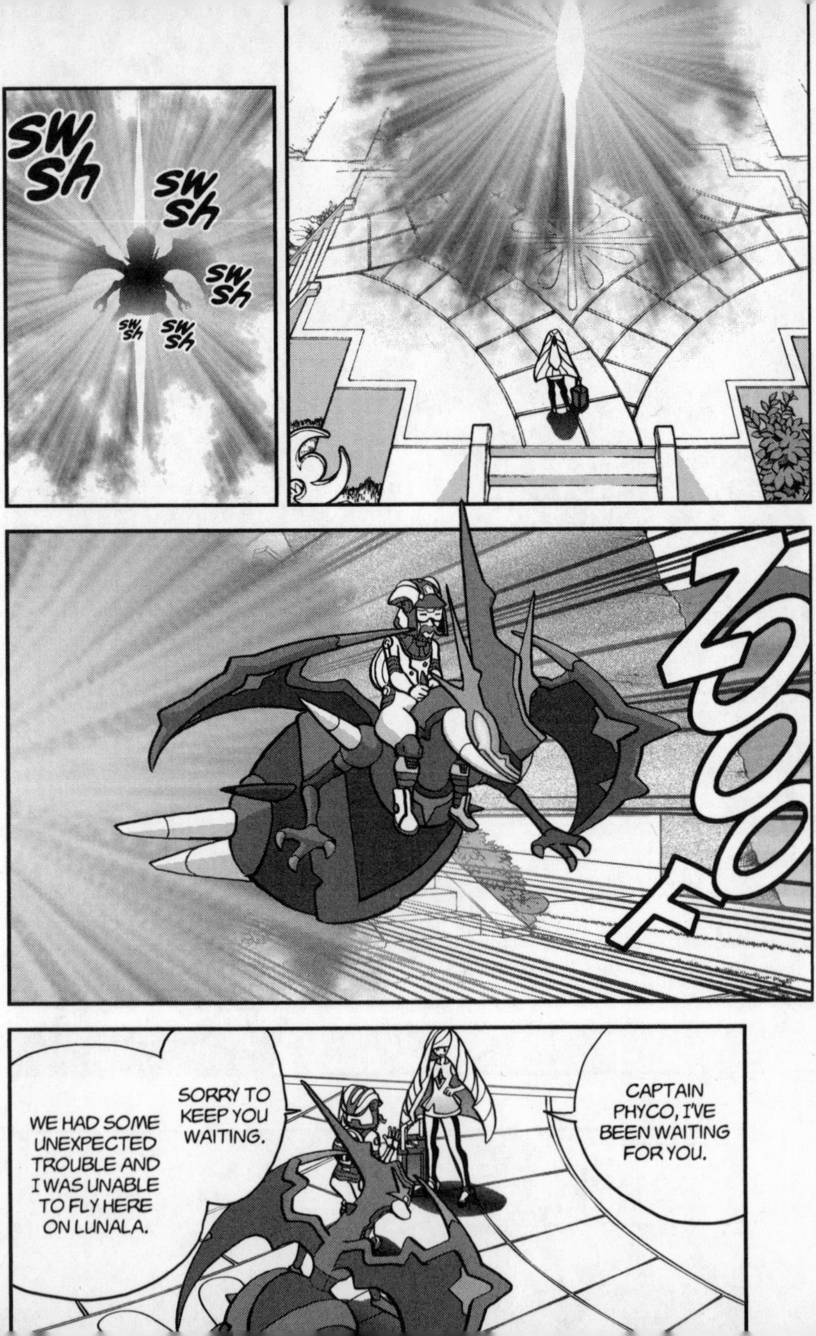
SWSH
SWSH
SWSH
SWSH
SWSH
ZOOOOF
CAPTAIN PHYCO, I'VE BEEN WAITING FOR YOU.
SORRY TO KEEP YOU WAITING.
WE HAD SOME UNEXPECTED TROUBLE AND I WAS UNABLE TO FLY HERE ON LUNALA.

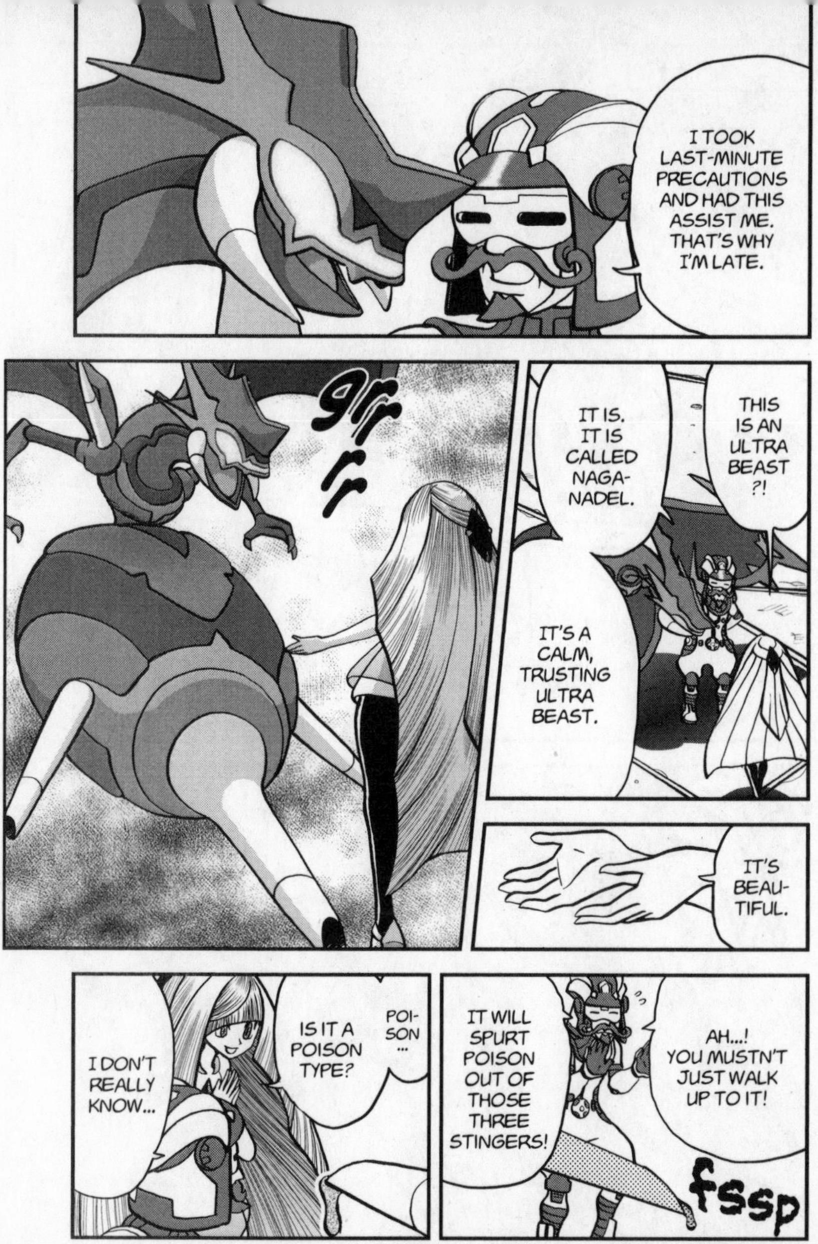
I TOOK LAST-MINUTE PRECAUTIONS AND HAD THIS ASSIST ME. THAT'S WHY I'M LATE.
THIS IS AN ULTRA BEAST ?!
IT IS. IT IS CALLED NAGA-NADEL.
IT'S A CALM, TRUSTING ULTRA BEAST.
IT'S BEAU-TIFUL.
grrr
AH...! YOU MUSTN'T JUST WALK UP TO IT!
IT WILL SPURT POISON OUT OF THOSE THREE STINGERS!
fssp
POI-SON ...
IS IT A POISON TYPE?
I DON'T REALLY KNOW...

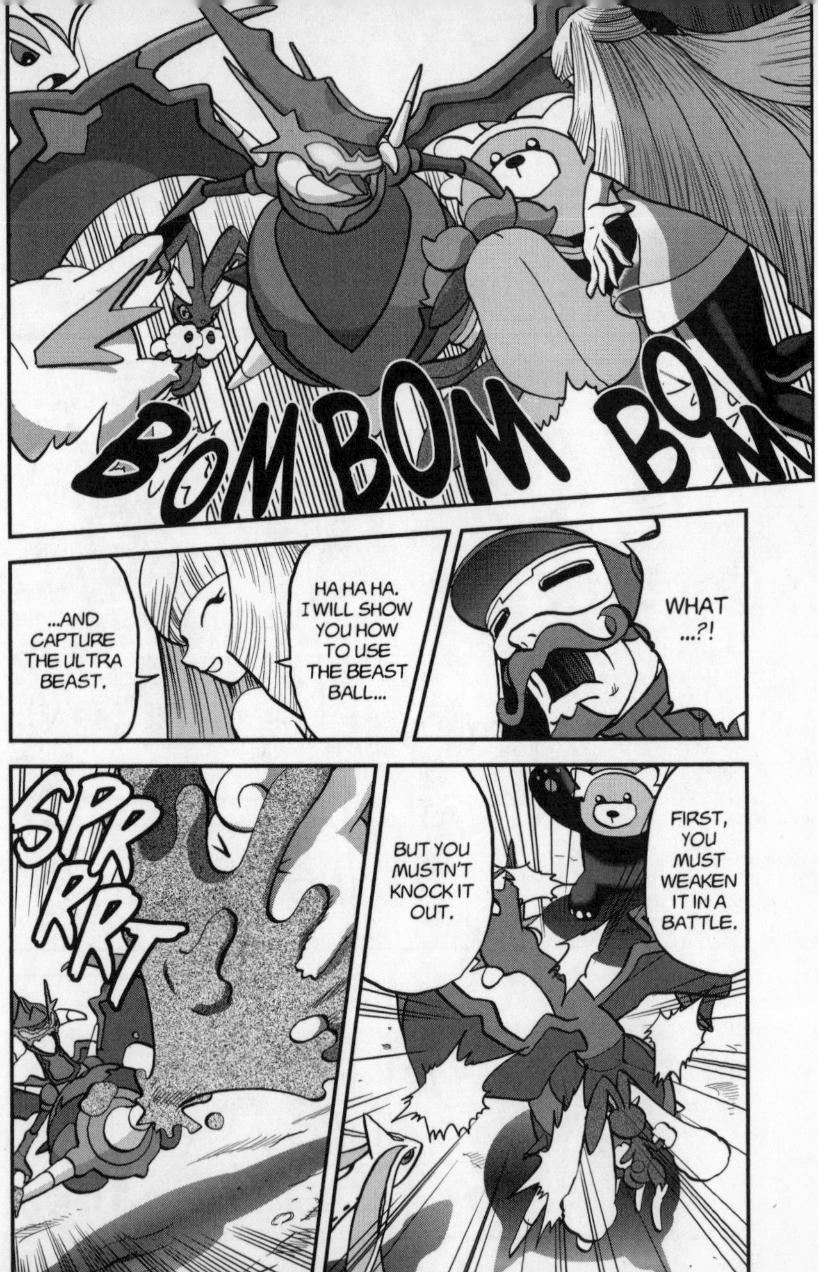
BOM BOM BOM
WHAT ...?!
HA HA HA. I WILL SHOW YOU HOW TO USE THE BEAST BALL...
...AND CAPTURE THE ULTRA BEAST.
FIRST, YOU MUST WEAKEN IT IN A BATTLE.
BUT YOU MUSTN'T KNOCK IT OUT.
SPRRRT

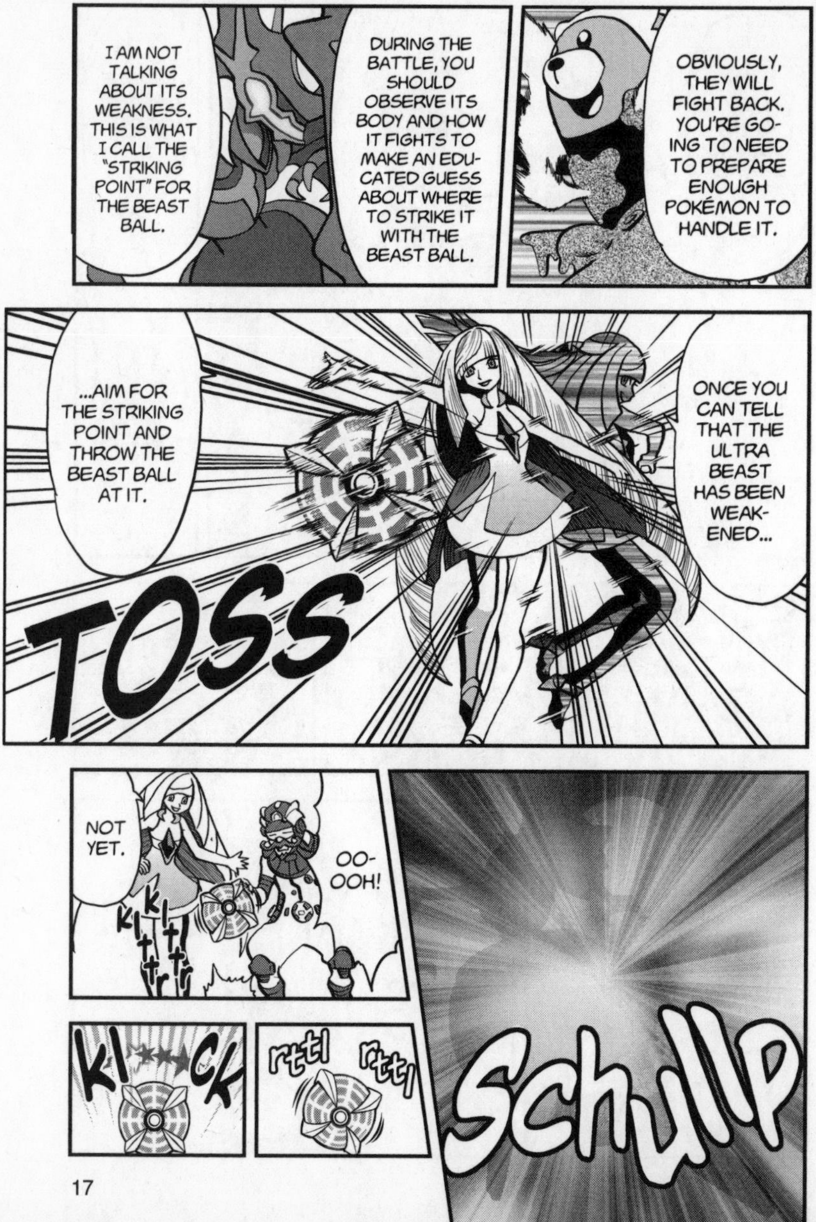
OBVIOUSLY, THEY WILL FIGHT BACK. YOU'RE GOING TO NEED TO PREPARE ENOUGH POKéMON TO HANDLE IT.
DURING THE BATTLE, YOU SHOULD OBSERVE ITS BODY AND HOW IT FIGHTS TO MAKE AN EDUCATED GUESS ABOUT WHERE TO STRIKE IT WITH THE BEAST BALL.
I AM NOT TALKING ABOUT ITS WEAKNESS. THIS IS WHAT I CALL THE "STRIKING POINT" FOR THE BEAST BALL.
ONCE YOU CAN TELL THAT THE ULTRA BEAST HAS BEEN WEAKENED...
...AIM FOR THE STRIKING POINT AND THROW THE BEAST BALL AT IT.
TOSS
Schullp
NOT YET.
OO-OOH!
Kl Kl ttrr ttrr
rttl rttl
Kl★★★Ck

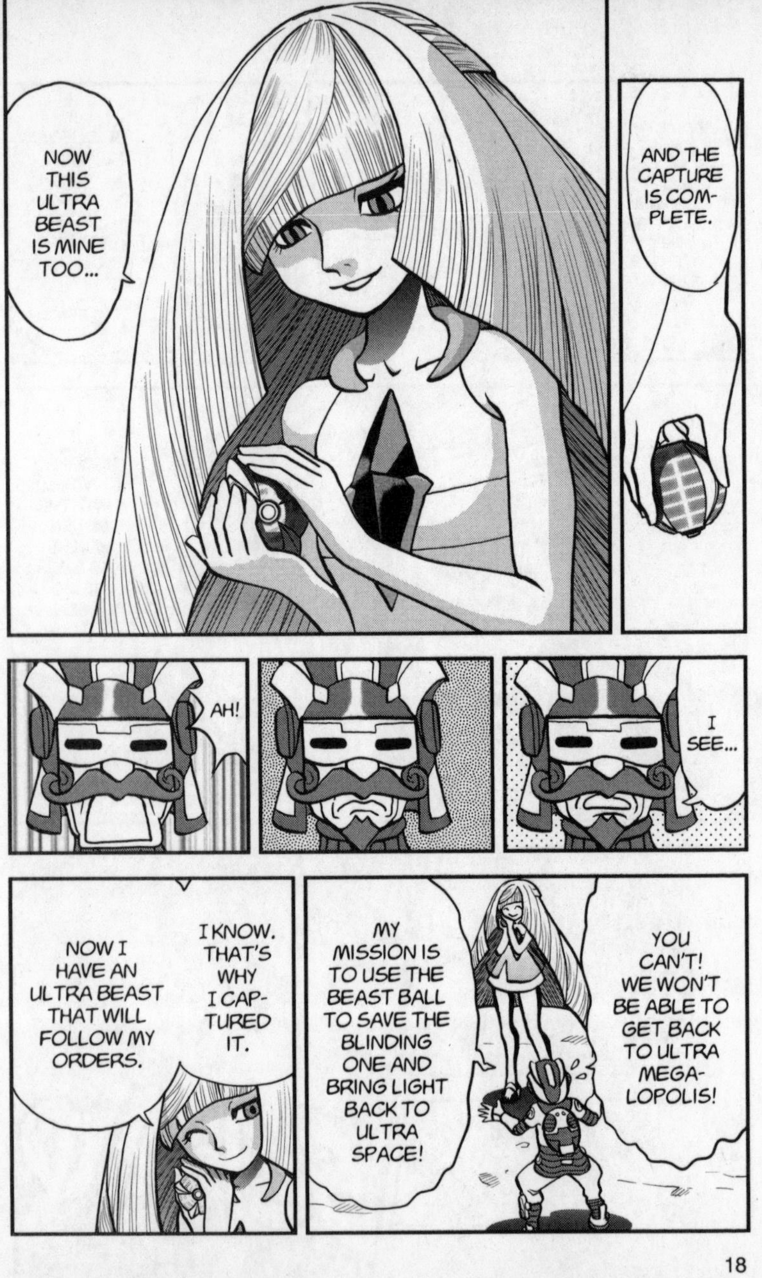
AND THE CAPTURE IS COMPLETE.
NOW THIS ULTRA BEAST IS MINE TOO...
I SEE...
AH!
YOU CAN'T! WE WON'T BE ABLE TO GET BACK TO ULTRA MEGALOPOLIS!
MY MISSION IS TO USE THE BEAST BALL TO SAVE THE BLINDING ONE AND BRING LIGHT BACK TO ULTRA SPACE!
I KNOW. THAT'S WHY I CAPTURED IT.
NOW I HAVE AN ULTRA BEAST THAT WILL FOLLOW MY ORDERS.

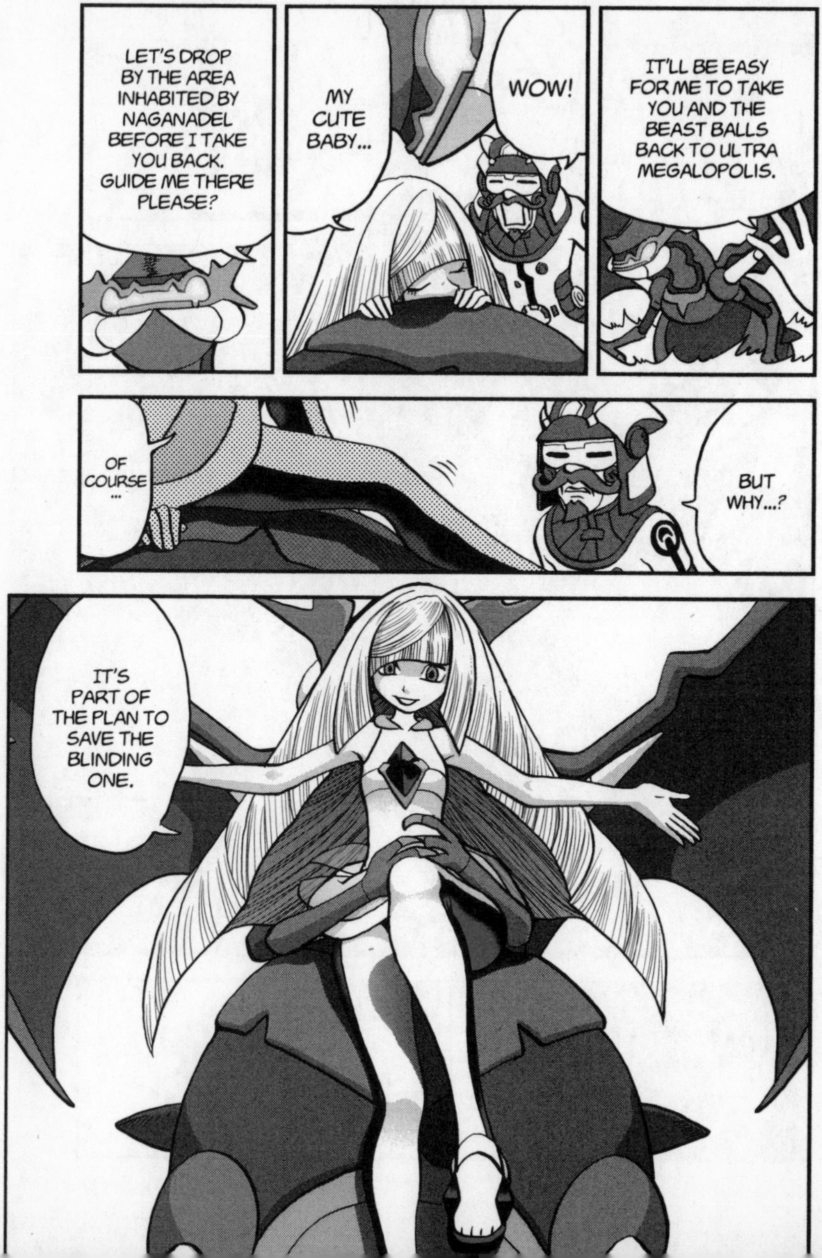
IT'LL BE EASY FOR ME TO TAKE YOU AND THE BEAST BALLS BACK TO ULTRA MEGALOPOLIS.
WOW!
MY CUTE BABY...
LET'S DROP BY THE AREA INHABITED BY NAGANADEL BEFORE I TAKE YOU BACK. GUIDE ME THERE PLEASE?
BUT WHY...?
OF COURSE...
IT'S PART OF THE PLAN TO SAVE THE BLINDING ONE.

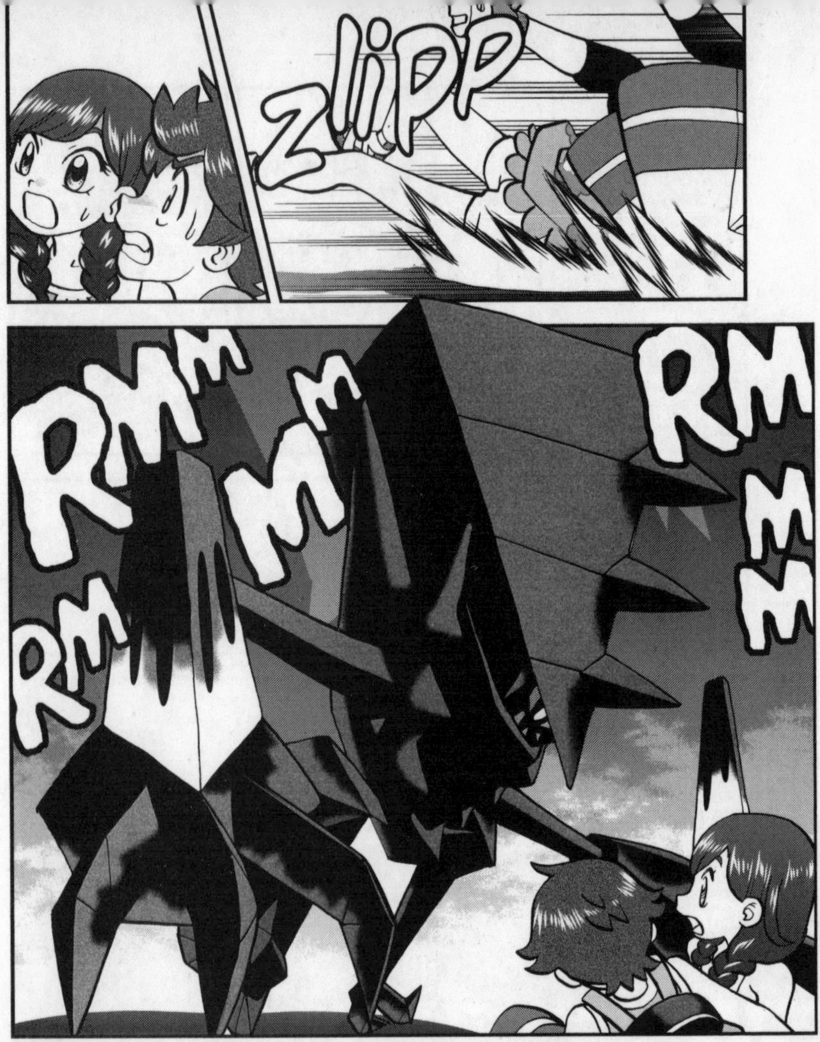
ZLIIPP
RMMMM
RMMM
MMM
RM
WHAT IS THIS GUY?!
THE BLINDING ONE.

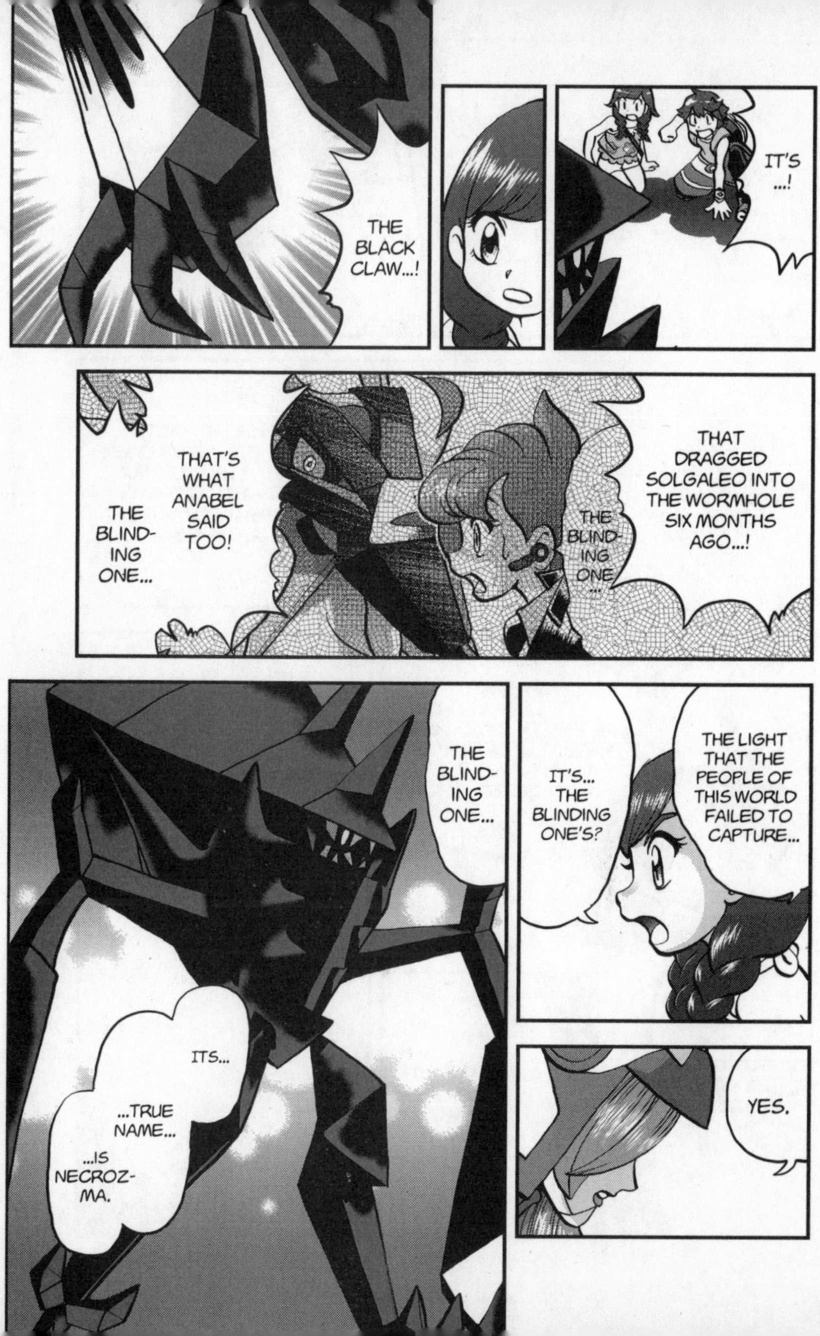
IT'S ...!
THE BLACK CLAW...!
THAT DRAGGED SOLGALEO INTO THE WORMHOLE SIX MONTHS AGO...!
THE BLINDING ONE...
THAT'S WHAT ANABEL SAID TOO!
THE BLINDING ONE...
THE LIGHT THAT THE PEOPLE OF THIS WORLD FAILED TO CAPTURE...
IT'S... THE BLINDING ONE'S?
YES.
THE BLINDING ONE...
ITS...
...TRUE NAME...
...IS NECROZMA.

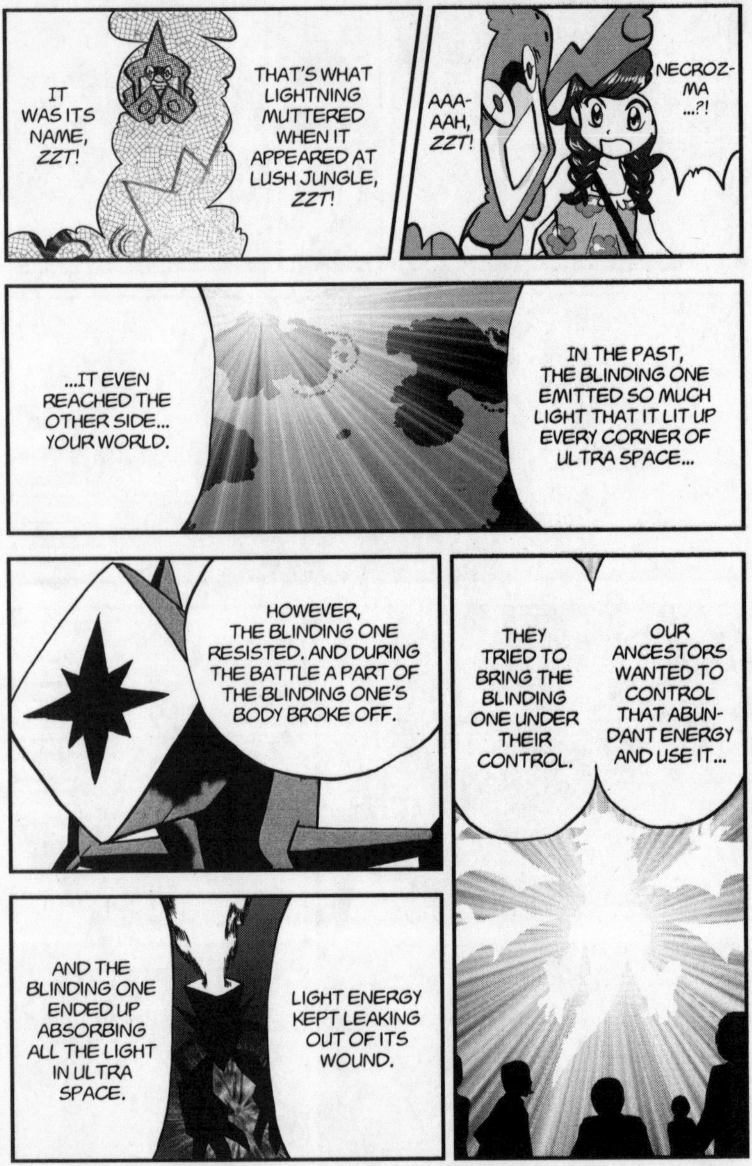
NECROZ-MA ...?!
AAA-AAH, ZZT!
THAT'S WHAT LIGHTNING MUTTERED WHEN IT APPEARED AT LUSH JUNGLE, ZZT!
IT WAS ITS NAME, ZZT!
IN THE PAST, THE BLINDING ONE EMITTED SO MUCH LIGHT THAT IT LIT UP EVERY CORNER OF ULTRA SPACE...
...IT EVEN REACHED THE OTHER SIDE... YOUR WORLD.
OUR ANCESTORS WANTED TO CONTROL THAT ABUN-DANT ENERGY AND USE IT...
THEY TRIED TO BRING THE BLINDING ONE UNDER THEIR CONTROL.
HOWEVER, THE BLINDING ONE RESISTED. AND DURING THE BATTLE A PART OF THE BLINDING ONE'S BODY BROKE OFF.
LIGHT ENERGY KEPT LEAKING OUT OF ITS WOUND.
AND THE BLINDING ONE ENDED UP ABSORBING ALL THE LIGHT IN ULTRA SPACE.

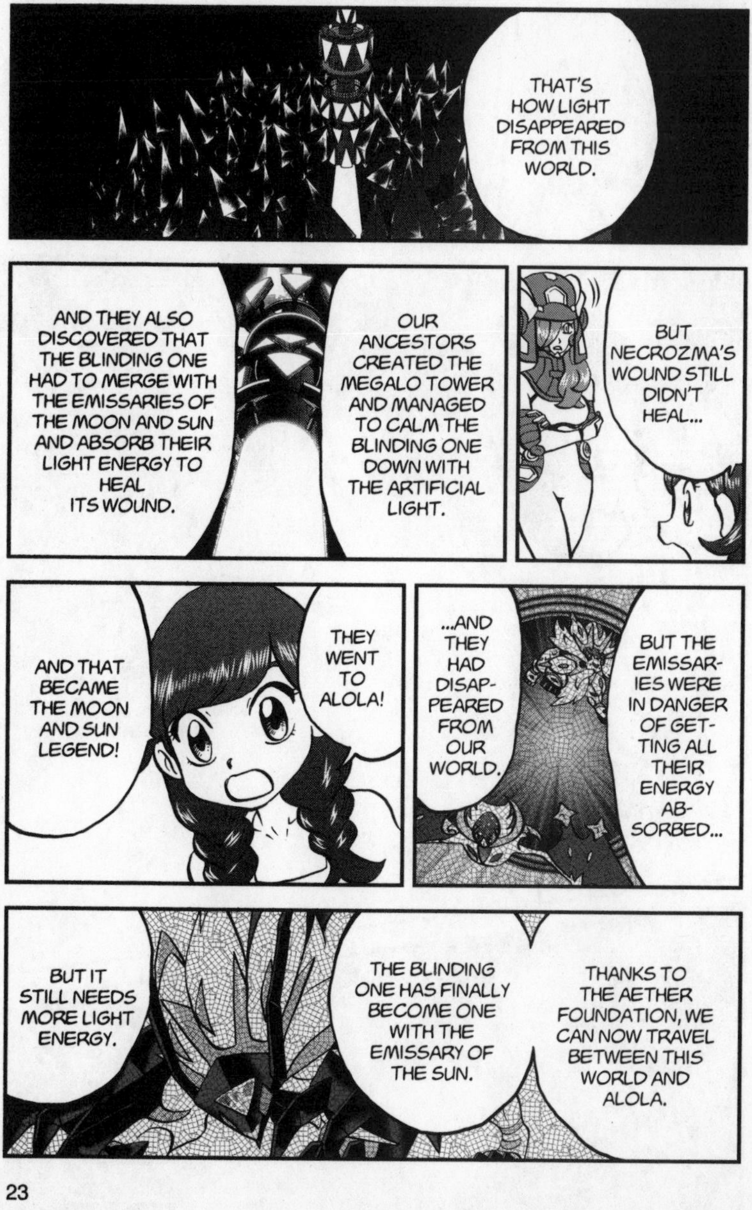
THAT'S HOW LIGHT DISAPPEARED FROM THIS WORLD.
BUT NECROZMA'S WOUND STILL DIDN'T HEAL...
OUR ANCESTORS CREATED THE MEGALO TOWER AND MANAGED TO CALM THE BLINDING ONE DOWN WITH THE ARTIFICIAL LIGHT.
AND THEY ALSO DISCOVERED THAT THE BLINDING ONE HAD TO MERGE WITH THE EMISSARIES OF THE MOON AND SUN AND ABSORB THEIR LIGHT ENERGY TO HEAL ITS WOUND.
BUT THE EMISSARIES WERE IN DANGER OF GETTING ALL THEIR ENERGY ABSORBED...
...AND THEY HAD DISAPPEARED FROM OUR WORLD.
THEY WENT TO ALOLA!
AND THAT BECAME THE MOON AND SUN LEGEND!
THANKS TO THE AETHER FOUNDATION, WE CAN NOW TRAVEL BETWEEN THIS WORLD AND ALOLA.
THE BLINDING ONE HAS FINALLY BECOME ONE WITH THE EMISSARY OF THE SUN.
BUT IT STILL NEEDS MORE LIGHT ENERGY.

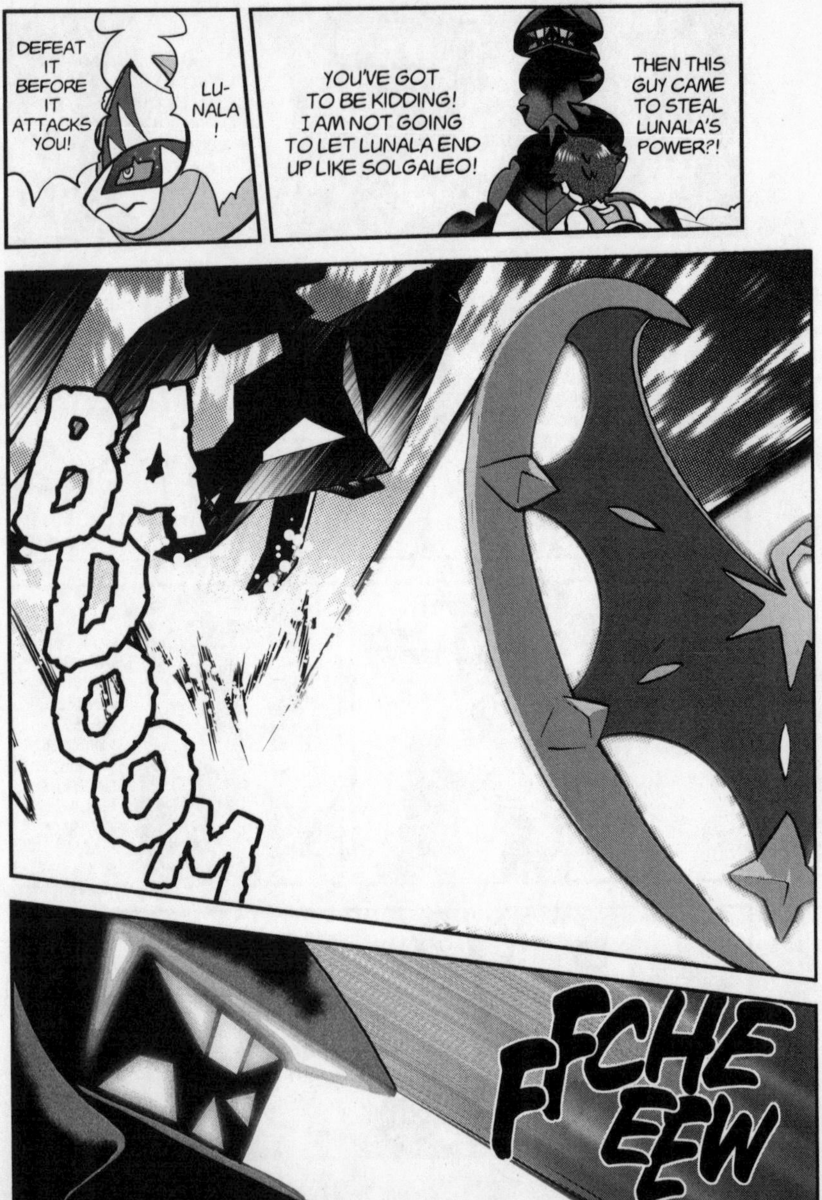
THEN THIS GUY CAME TO STEAL LUNALA'S POWER?!
YOU'VE GOT TO BE KIDDING! I AM NOT GOING TO LET LUNALA END UP LIKE SOLGALEO!
LU-NALA!
DEFEAT IT BEFORE IT ATTACKS YOU!
BADOOM
FFCHEEEW

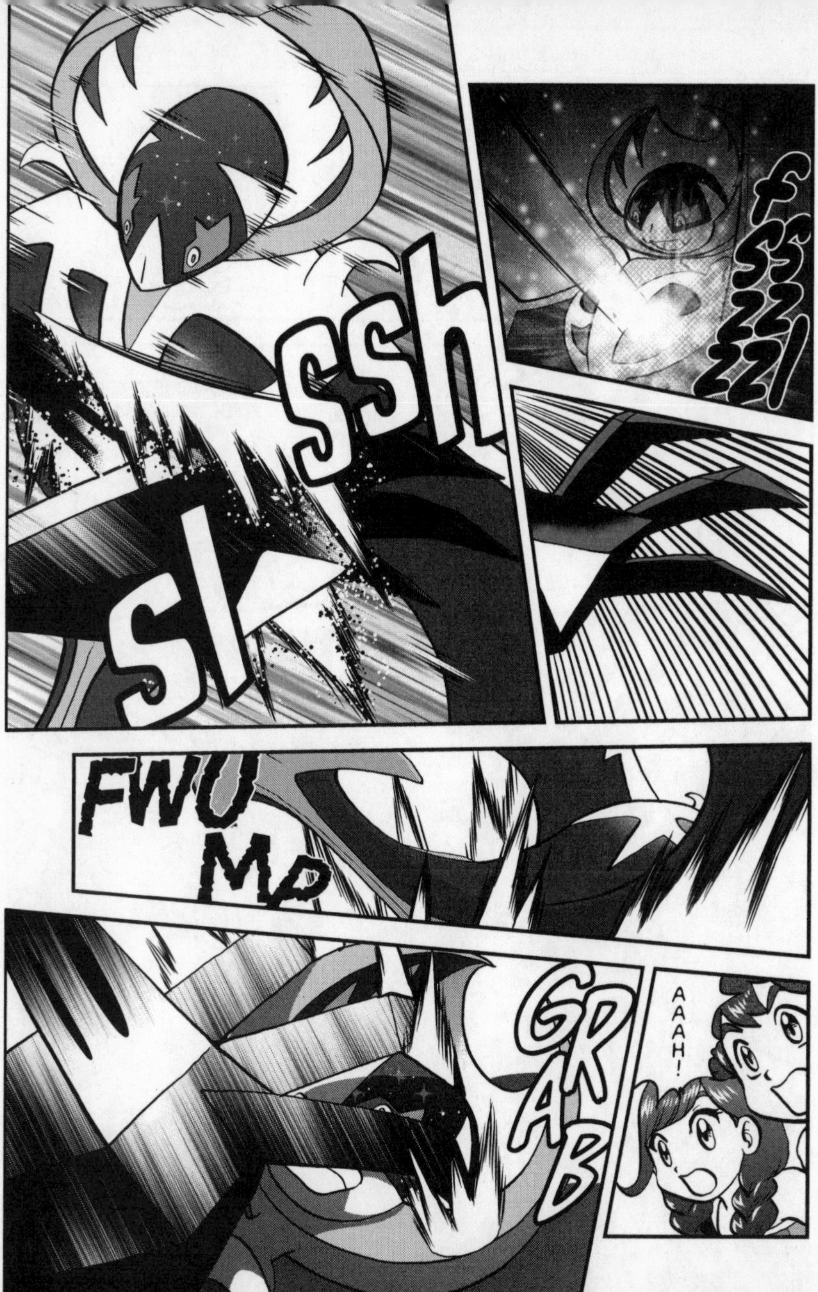
fSSZZZl
sl
ssh
FWUMP
AAAH!
GRAB

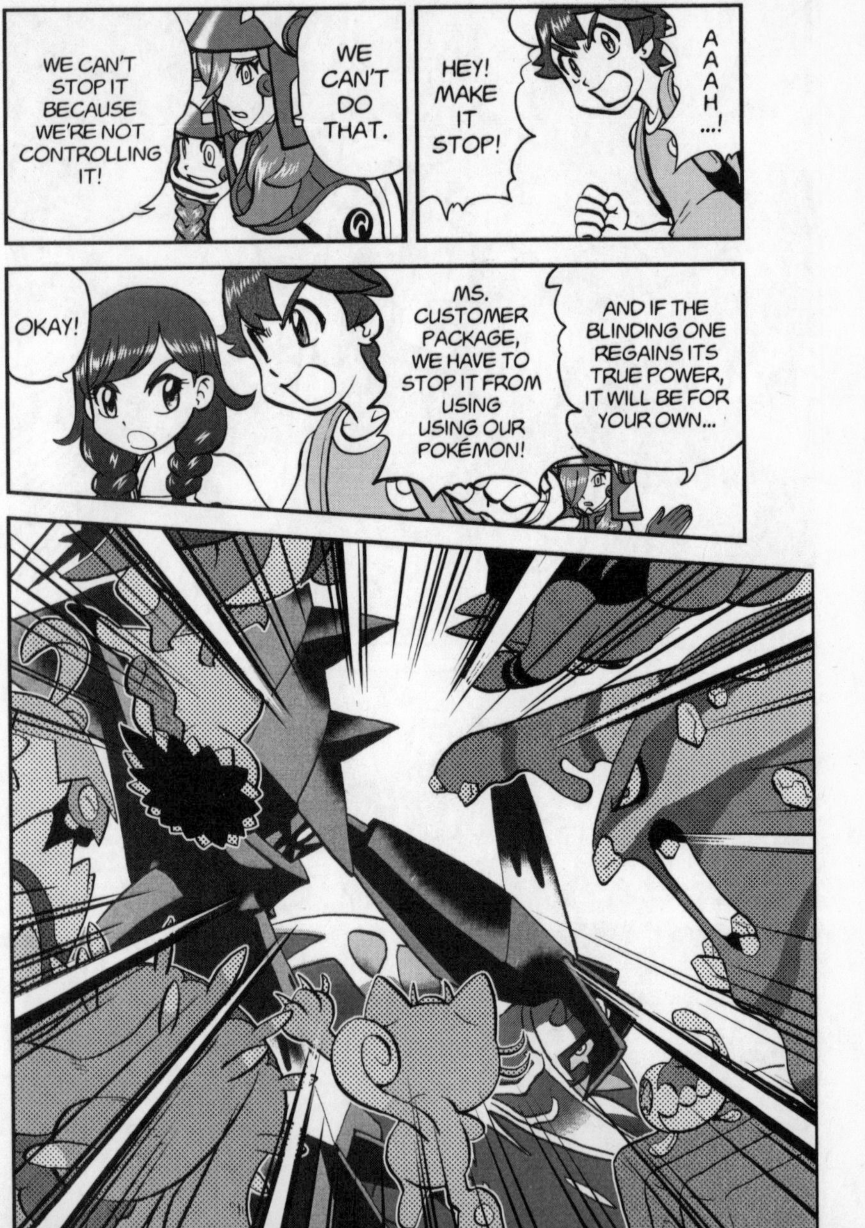
AAAAH...!
HEY! MAKE IT STOP!
WE CAN'T DO THAT.
WE CAN'T STOP IT BECAUSE WE'RE NOT CONTROLLING IT!
AND IF THE BLINDING ONE REGAINS ITS TRUE POWER, IT WILL BE FOR YOUR OWN...
MS. CUSTOMER PACKAGE, WE HAVE TO STOP IT FROM USING USING OUR POKÉMON!
OKAY!

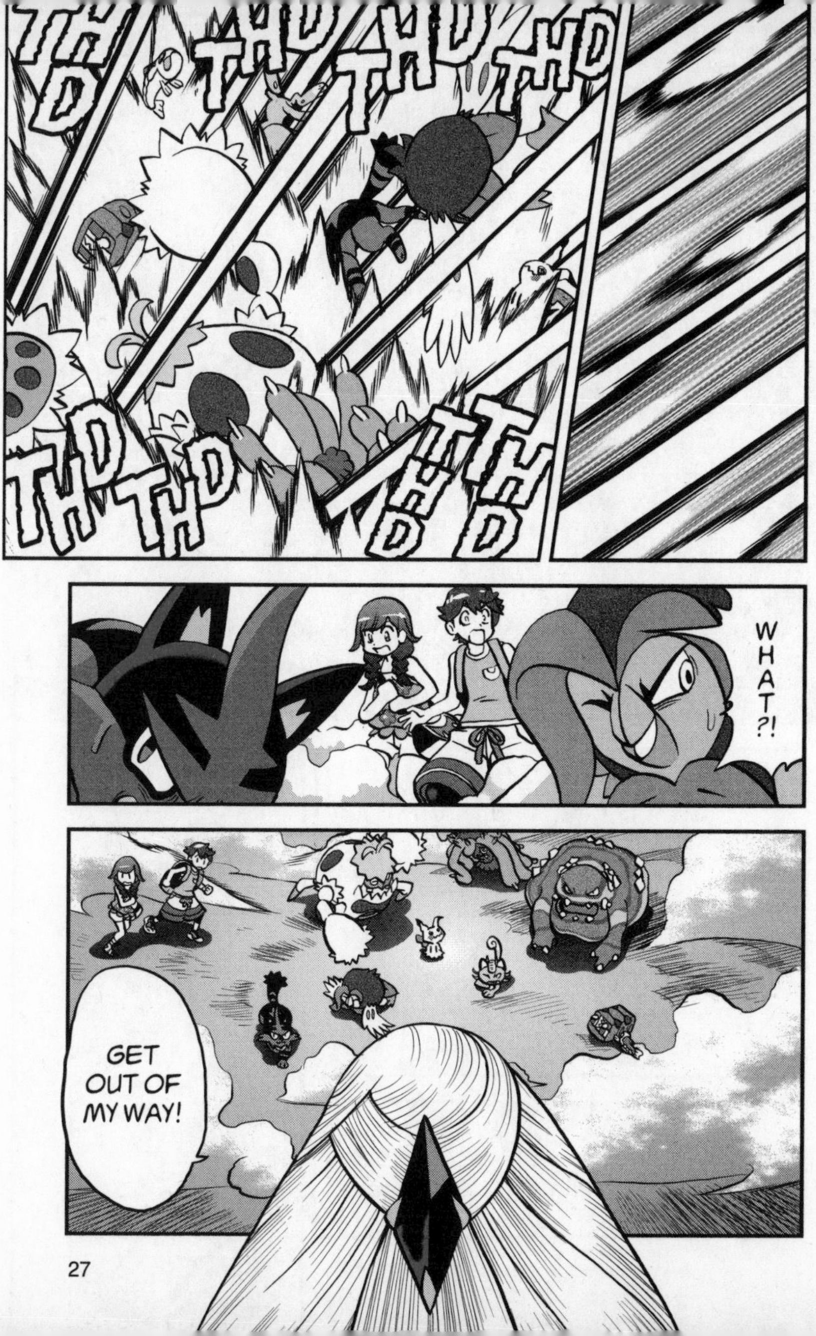
THD
THD
THD
THD
THD
THD
THD
THD
WHAT?!
GET OUT OF MY WAY!

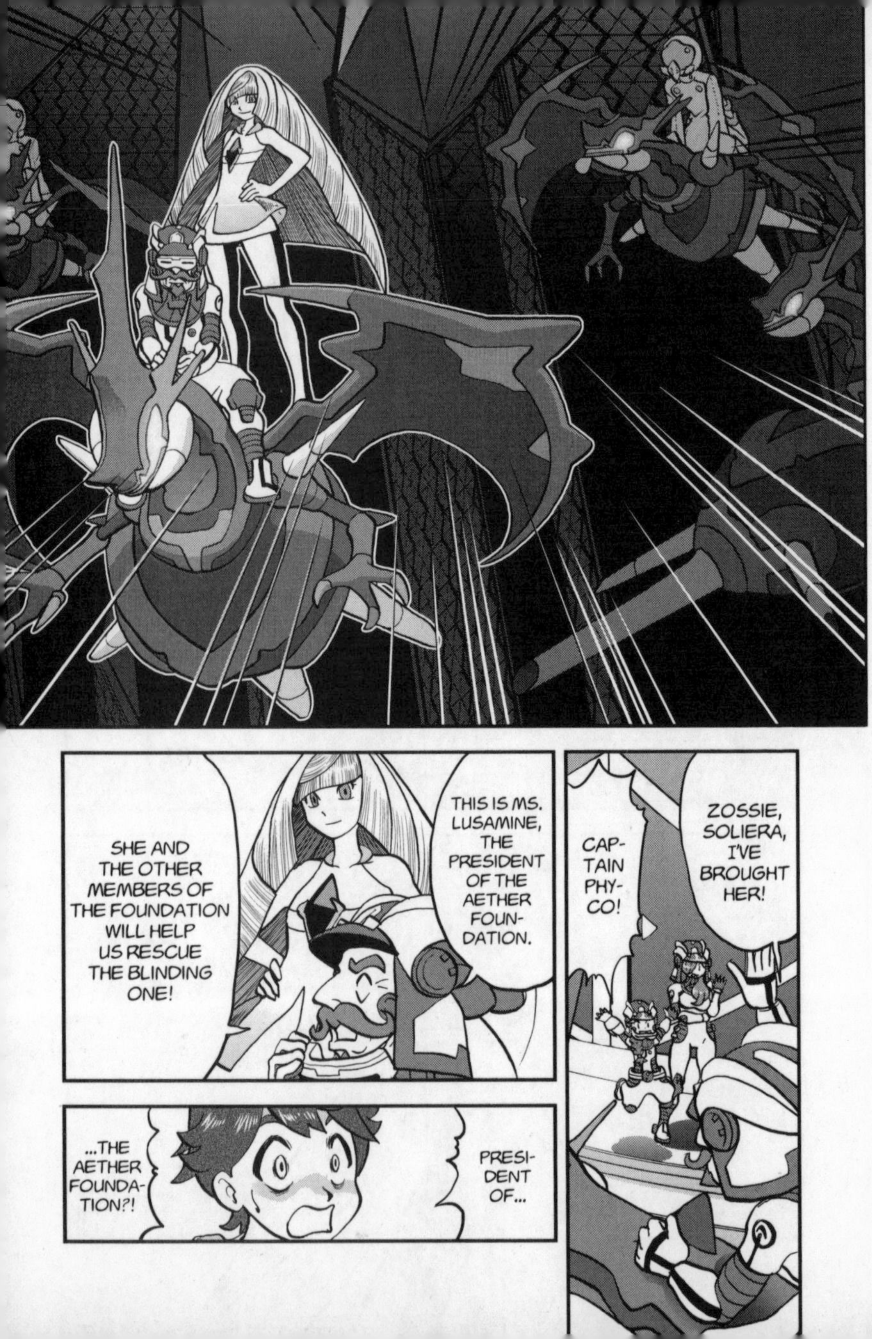
ZOSSIE, SOLIERA, I'VE BROUGHT HER!
CAP-TAIN PHY-CO!
THIS IS MS. LUSAMINE, THE PRESIDENT OF THE AETHER FOUN-DATION.
SHE AND THE OTHER MEMBERS OF THE FOUNDATION WILL HELP US RESCUE THE BLINDING ONE!
PRESI-DENT OF...
...THE AETHER FOUNDA-TION?!

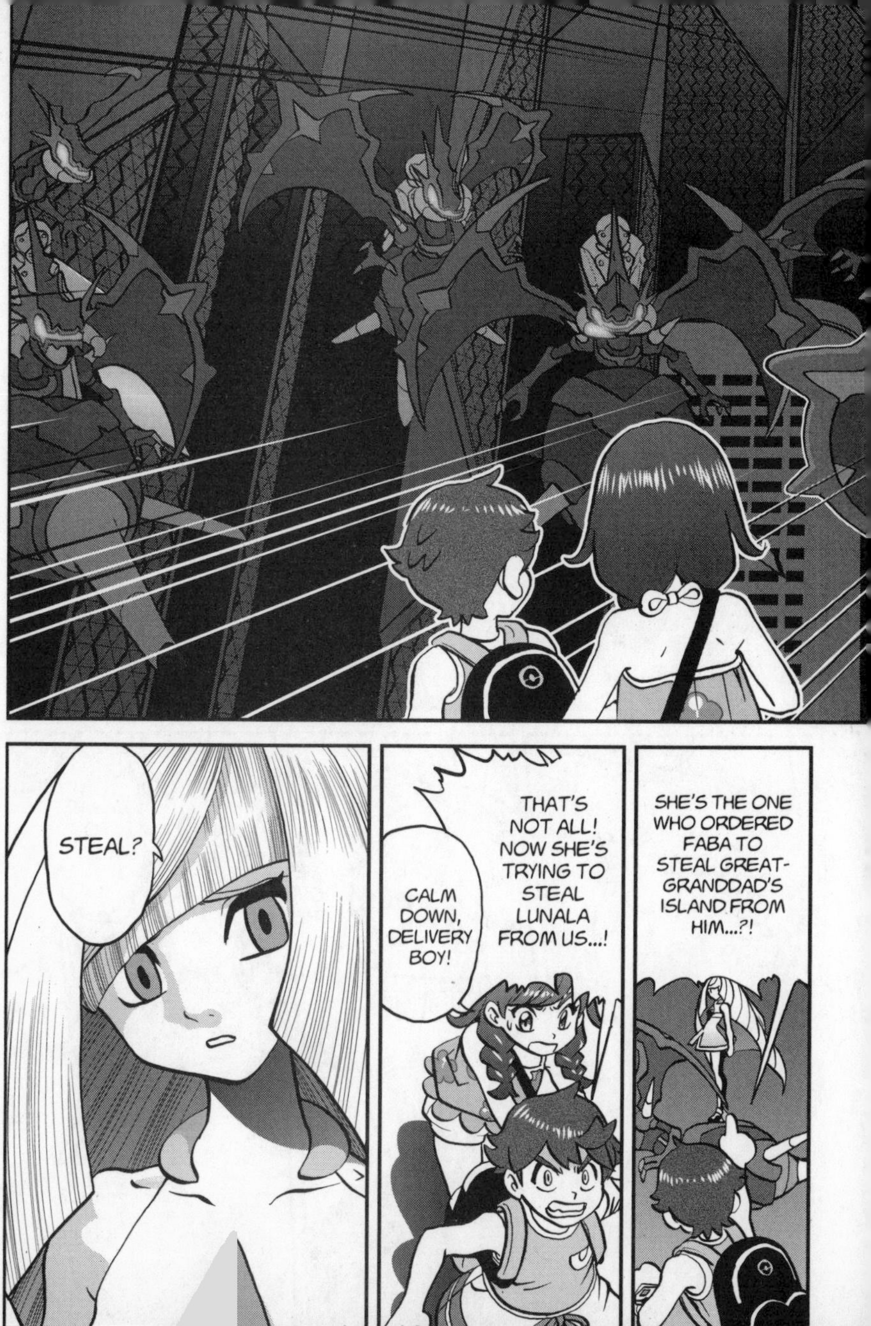
SHE'S THE ONE WHO ORDERED FABA TO STEAL GREAT-GRANDDAD'S ISLAND FROM HIM...?!
THAT'S NOT ALL! NOW SHE'S TRYING TO STEAL LUNALA FROM US...!
CALM DOWN, DELIVERY BOY!
STEAL?

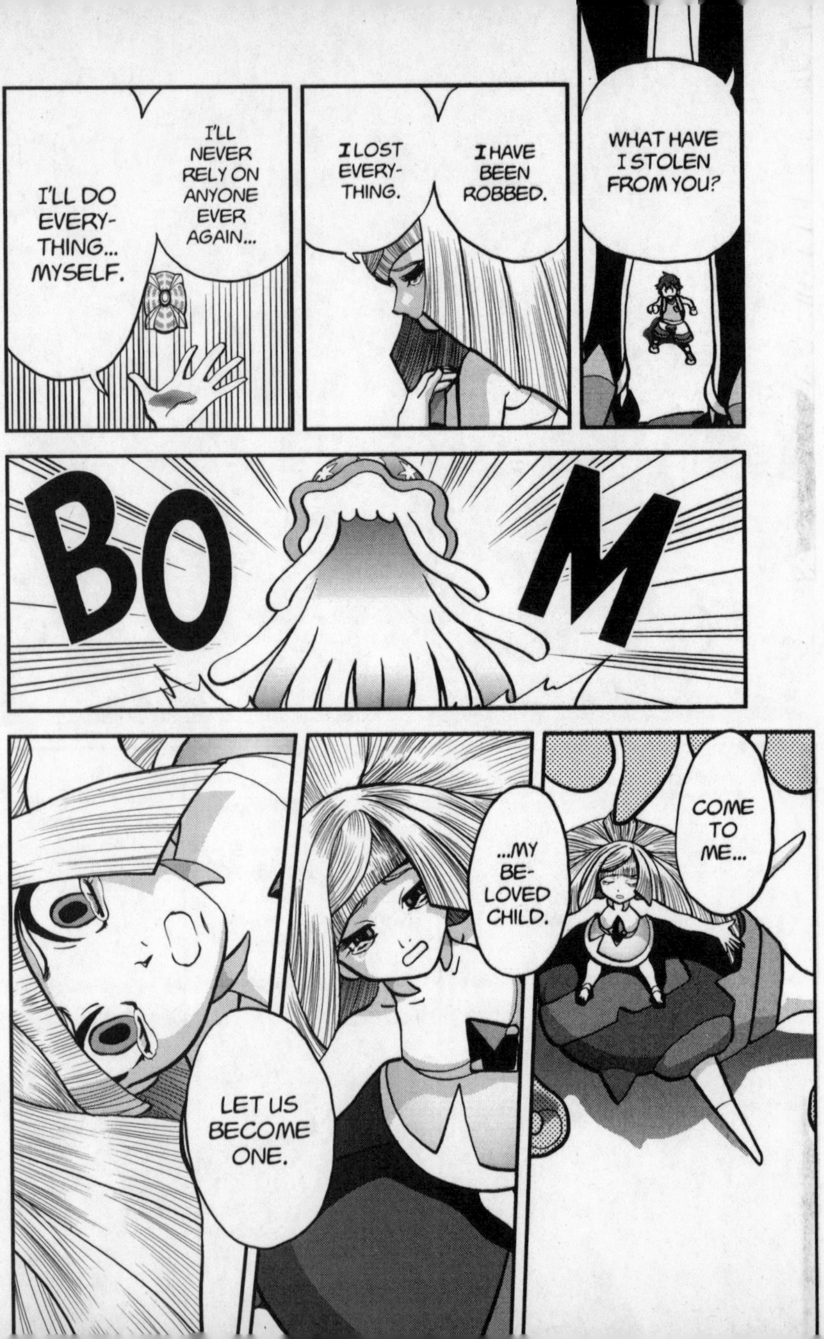
WHAT HAVE I STOLEN FROM YOU?
I HAVE BEEN ROBBED.
I LOST EVERY-THING.
I'LL NEVER RELY ON ANYONE EVER AGAIN...
I'LL DO EVERY-THING... MYSELF.
BO M
COME TO ME...
...MY BE-LOVED CHILD.
LET US BECOME ONE.

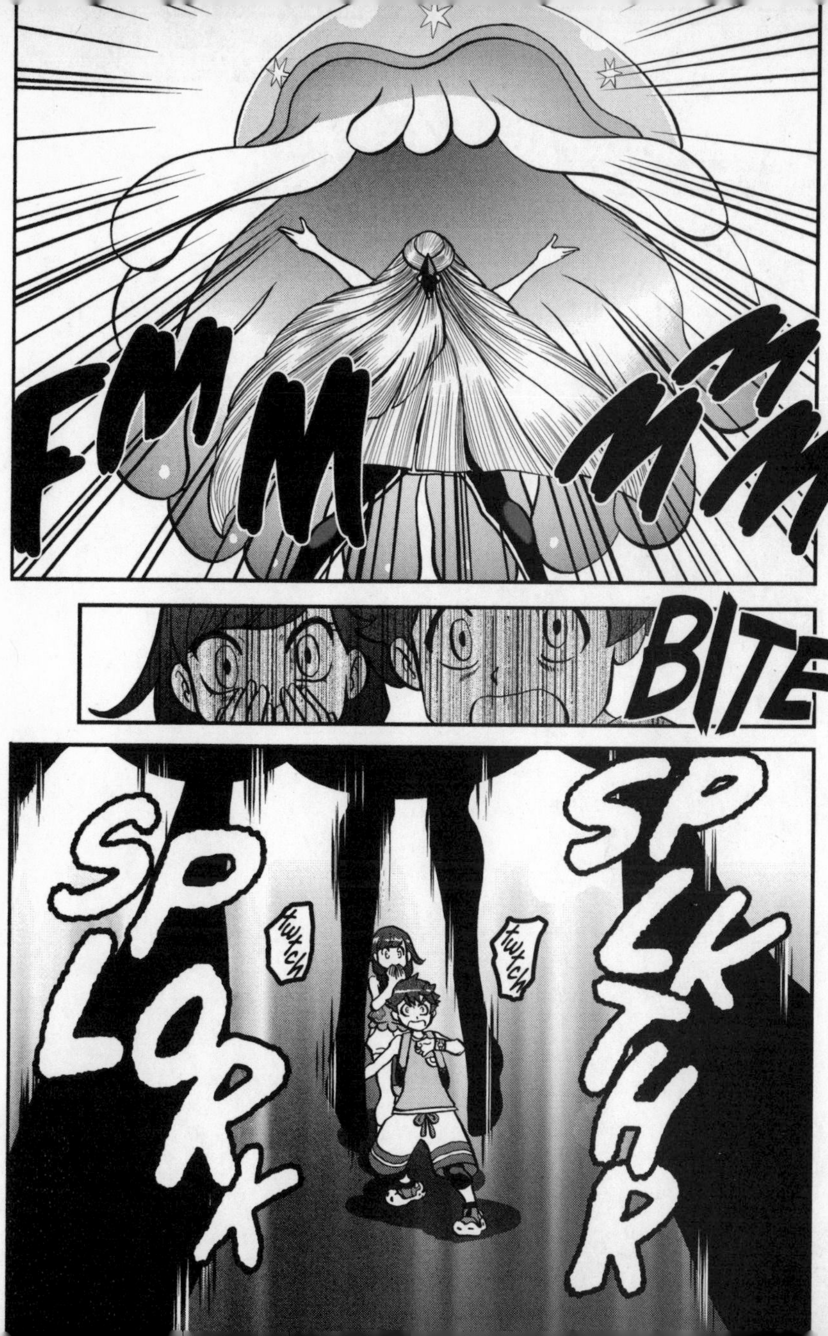
FMM
MMMMMM
BITE
SPLKTHR
twitch
twitch
SPLORK

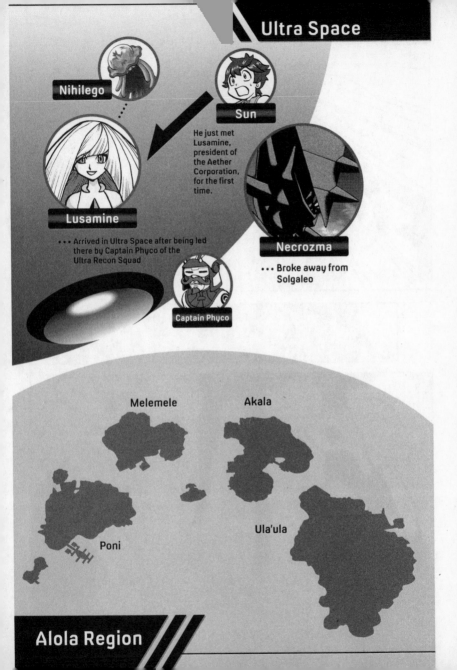

Ultra Space

Nihilego

Sun

He just met Lusamine, president of the Aether Corporation, for the first time.

Lusamine

••• Arrived in Ultra Space after being led there by Captain Phyco of the Ultra Recon Squad

Captain Phyco

Necrozma

••• Broke away from Solgaleo

Melemele

Akala

Poni

Ula'ula

Alola Region

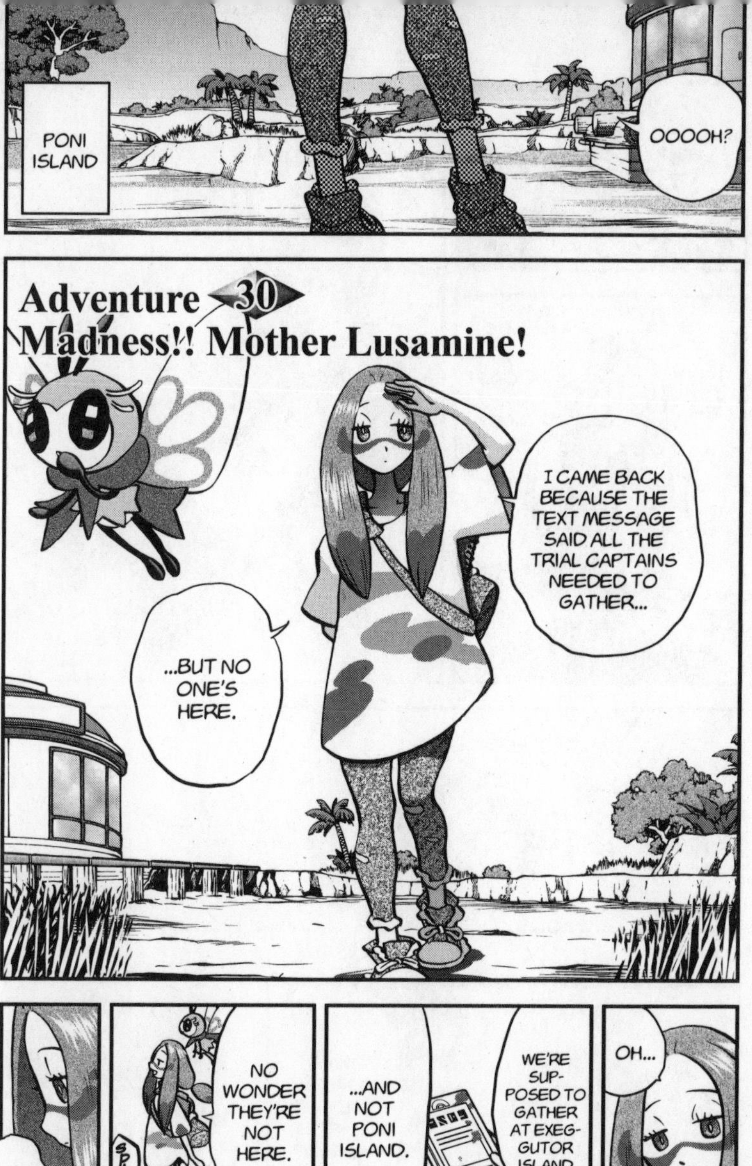
OOOOH?
PONI ISLAND
Adventure 30
Madness!! Mother Lusamine!
I CAME BACK BECAUSE THE TEXT MESSAGE SAID ALL THE TRIAL CAPTAINS NEEDED TO GATHER...
...BUT NO ONE'S HERE.
OH...
WE'RE SUP-POSED TO GATHER AT EXEG-GUTOR ISLAND ...
...AND NOT PONI ISLAND.
NO WONDER THEY'RE NOT HERE.
SPLIKK
URGH ...

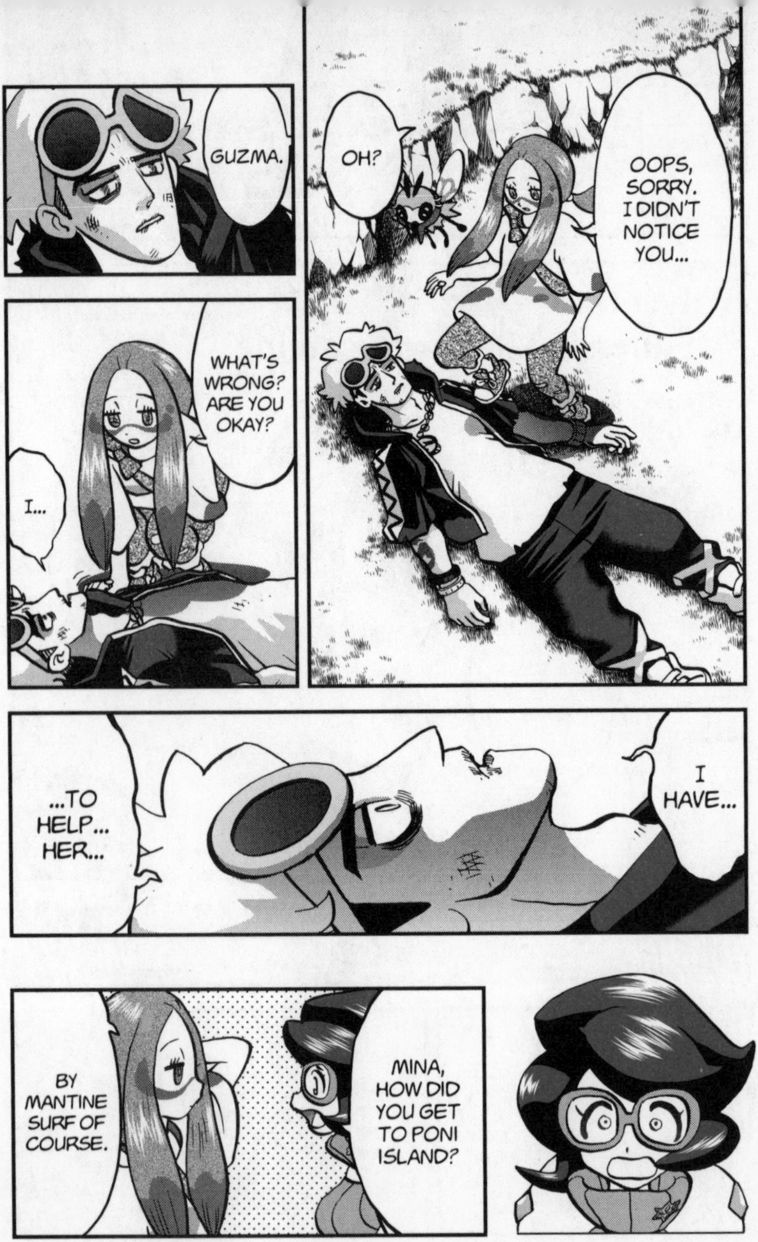
OOPS, SORRY. I DIDN'T NOTICE YOU...
OH?
GUZMA.
WHAT'S WRONG? ARE YOU OKAY?
I...
I HAVE...
...TO HELP... HER...
MINA, HOW DID YOU GET TO PONI ISLAND?
BY MANTINE SURF OF COURSE.

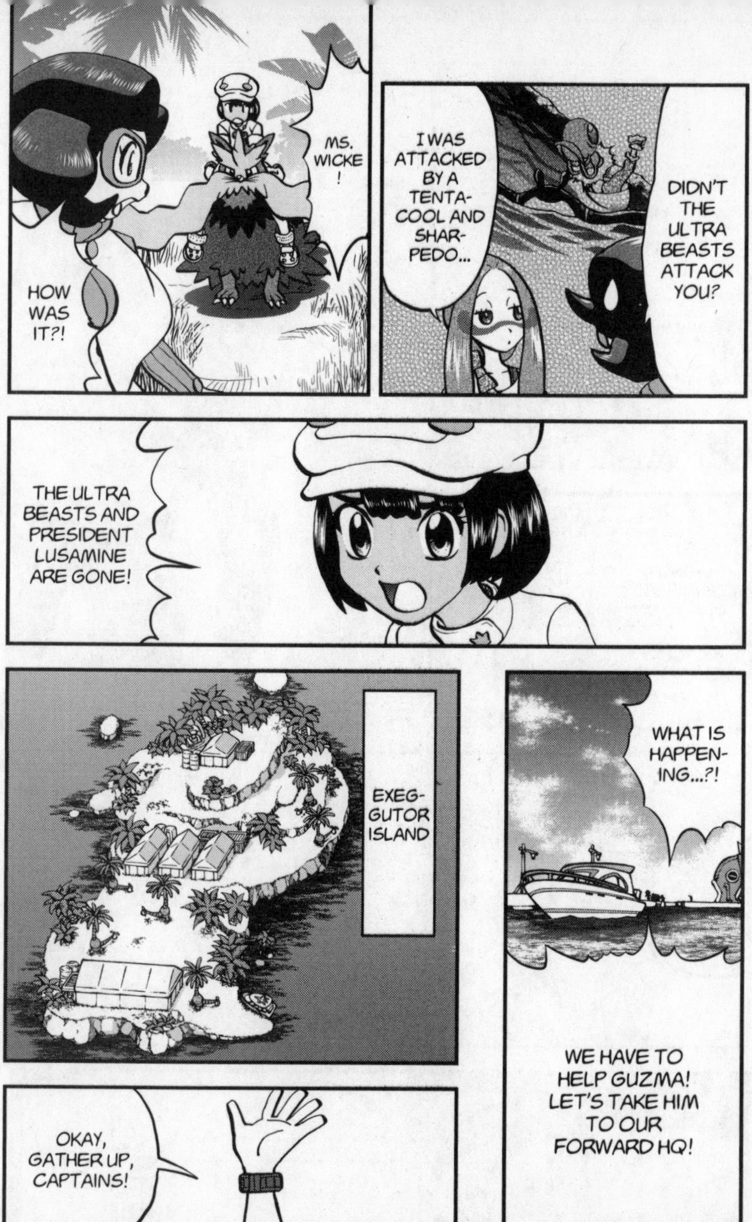
DIDN'T THE ULTRA BEASTS ATTACK YOU?
I WAS ATTACKED BY A TENTA-COOL AND SHAR-PEDO...
MS. WICKE!
HOW WAS IT?!
THE ULTRA BEASTS AND PRESIDENT LUSAMINE ARE GONE!
WHAT IS HAPPEN-ING...?!
WE HAVE TO HELP GUZMA! LET'S TAKE HIM TO OUR FORWARD HQ!
EXEG-GUTOR ISLAND
OKAY, GATHER UP, CAPTAINS!

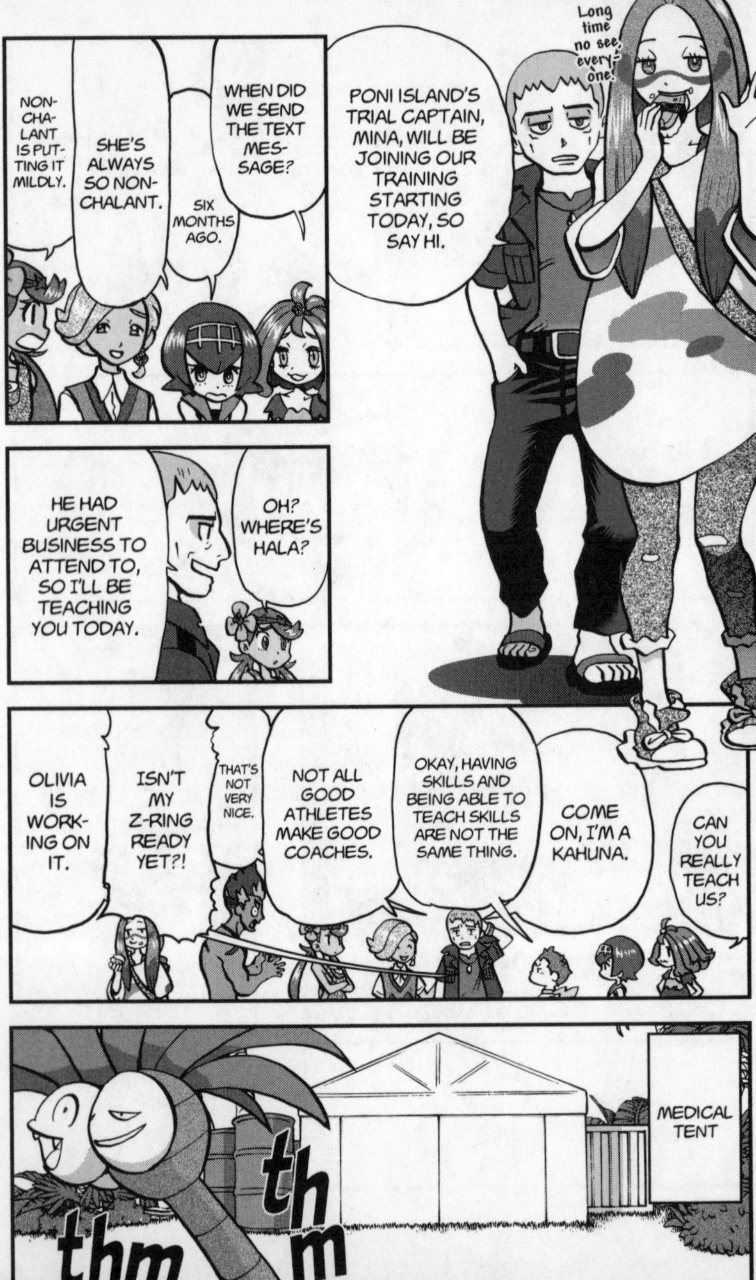
Long time no see, every-one!
PONI ISLAND'S TRIAL CAPTAIN, MINA, WILL BE JOINING OUR TRAINING STARTING TODAY, SO SAY HI.
WHEN DID WE SEND THE TEXT MES-SAGE?
SIX MONTHS AGO.
SHE'S ALWAYS SO NON-CHALANT.
NON-CHA-LANT IS PUT-TING IT MILDLY.
OH? WHERE'S HALA?
HE HAD URGENT BUSINESS TO ATTEND TO, SO I'LL BE TEACHING YOU TODAY.
CAN YOU REALLY TEACH US?
COME ON, I'M A KAHUNA.
OKAY, HAVING SKILLS AND BEING ABLE TO TEACH SKILLS ARE NOT THE SAME THING.
NOT ALL GOOD ATHLETES MAKE GOOD COACHES.
THAT'S NOT VERY NICE.
ISN'T MY Z-RING READY YET?!
OLIVIA IS WORKING ON IT.
MEDICAL TENT
th m
thm

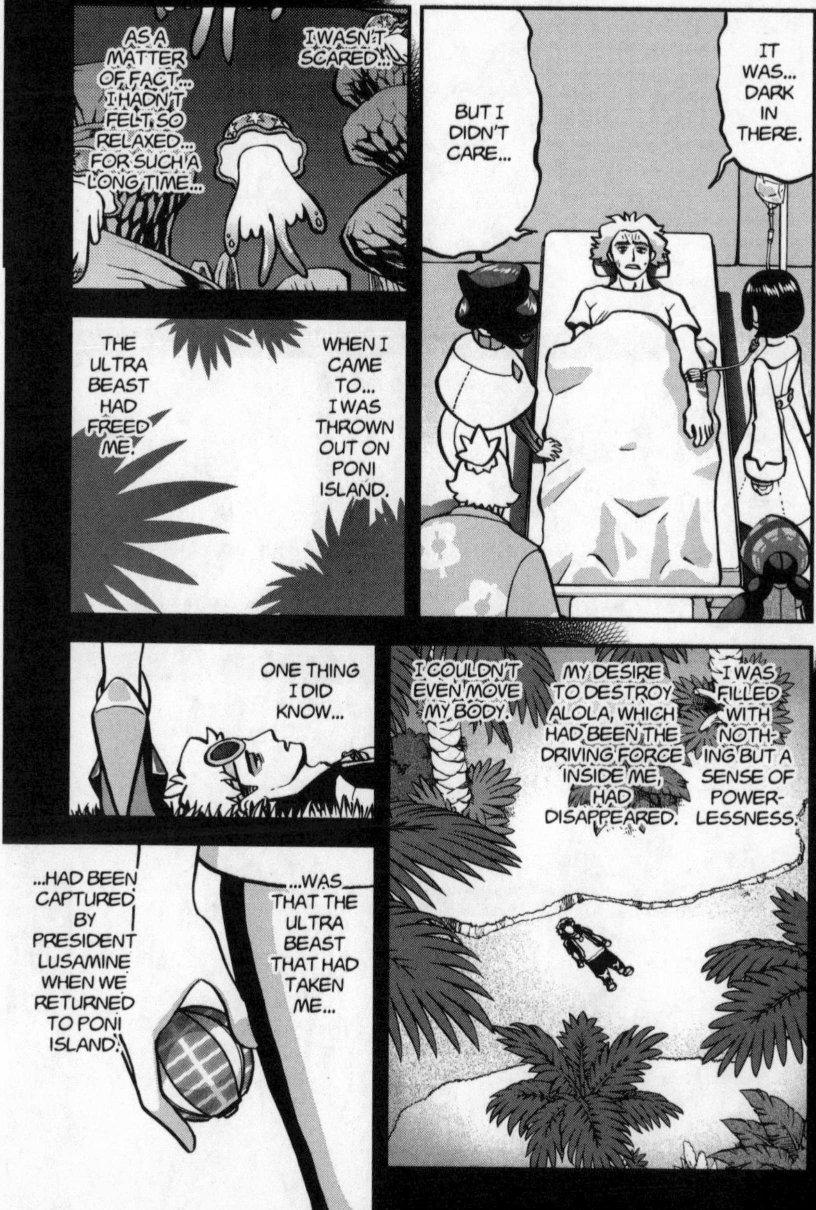
IT WAS... DARK IN THERE.
BUT I DIDN'T CARE...
I WASN'T SCARED...
AS A MATTER OF FACT... I HADN'T FELT SO RELAXED... FOR SUCH A LONG TIME...
WHEN I CAME TO... I WAS THROWN OUT ON PONI ISLAND.
THE ULTRA BEAST HAD FREED ME.
I WAS FILLED WITH NOTH-ING BUT A SENSE OF POWER-LESSNESS.
MY DESIRE TO DESTROY ALOLA, WHICH HAD BEEN THE DRIVING FORCE INSIDE ME, HAD DISAPPEARED.
I COULDN'T EVEN MOVE MY BODY.
ONE THING I DID KNOW...
...WAS THAT THE ULTRA BEAST THAT HAD TAKEN ME...
...HAD BEEN CAPTURED BY PRESIDENT LUSAMINE WHEN WE RETURNED TO PONI ISLAND.

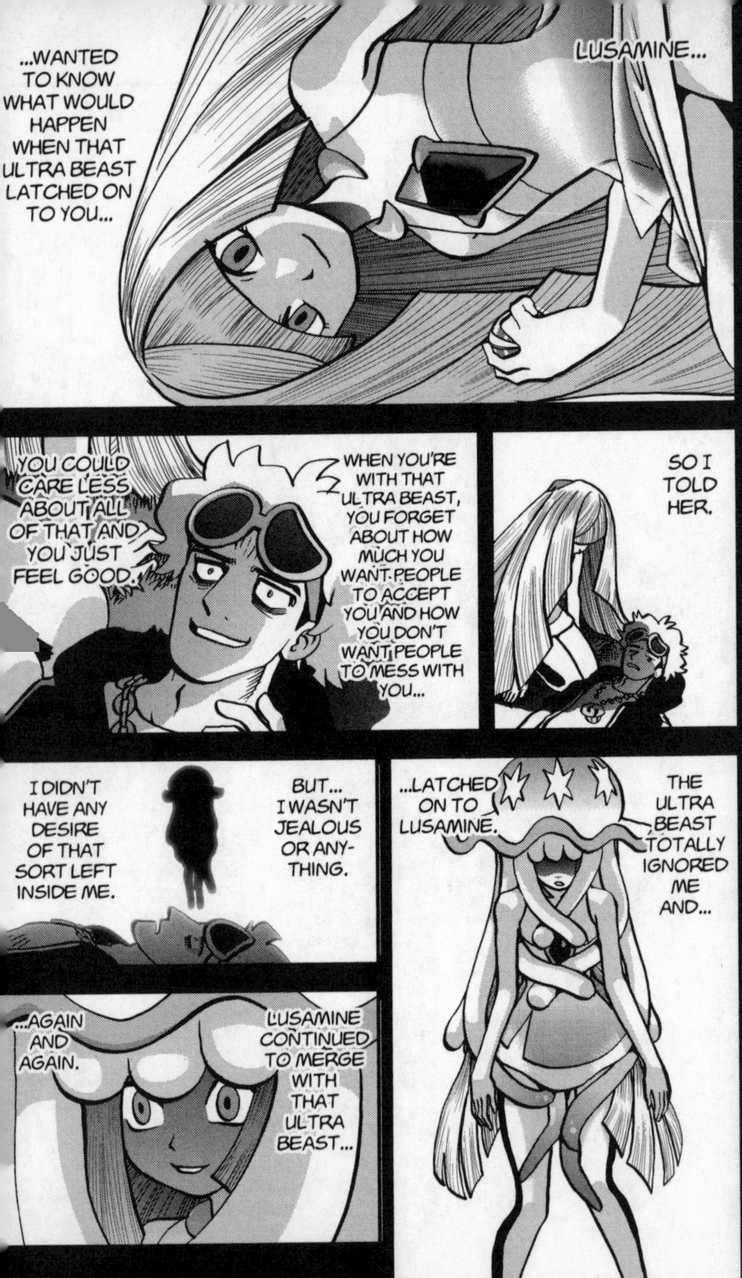
LUSAMINE...
...WANTED TO KNOW WHAT WOULD HAPPEN WHEN THAT ULTRA BEAST LATCHED ON TO YOU...
SO I TOLD HER.
WHEN YOU'RE WITH THAT ULTRA BEAST, YOU FORGET ABOUT HOW MUCH YOU WANT PEOPLE TO ACCEPT YOU AND HOW YOU DON'T WANT PEOPLE TO MESS WITH YOU...
YOU COULD CARE LESS ABOUT ALL OF THAT AND YOU JUST FEEL GOOD.
THE ULTRA BEAST TOTALLY IGNORED ME AND...
...LATCHED ON TO LUSAMINE.
BUT... I WASN'T JEALOUS OR ANY-THING.
I DIDN'T HAVE ANY DESIRE OF THAT SORT LEFT INSIDE ME.
LUSAMINE CONTINUED TO MERGE WITH THAT ULTRA BEAST...
...AGAIN AND AGAIN.

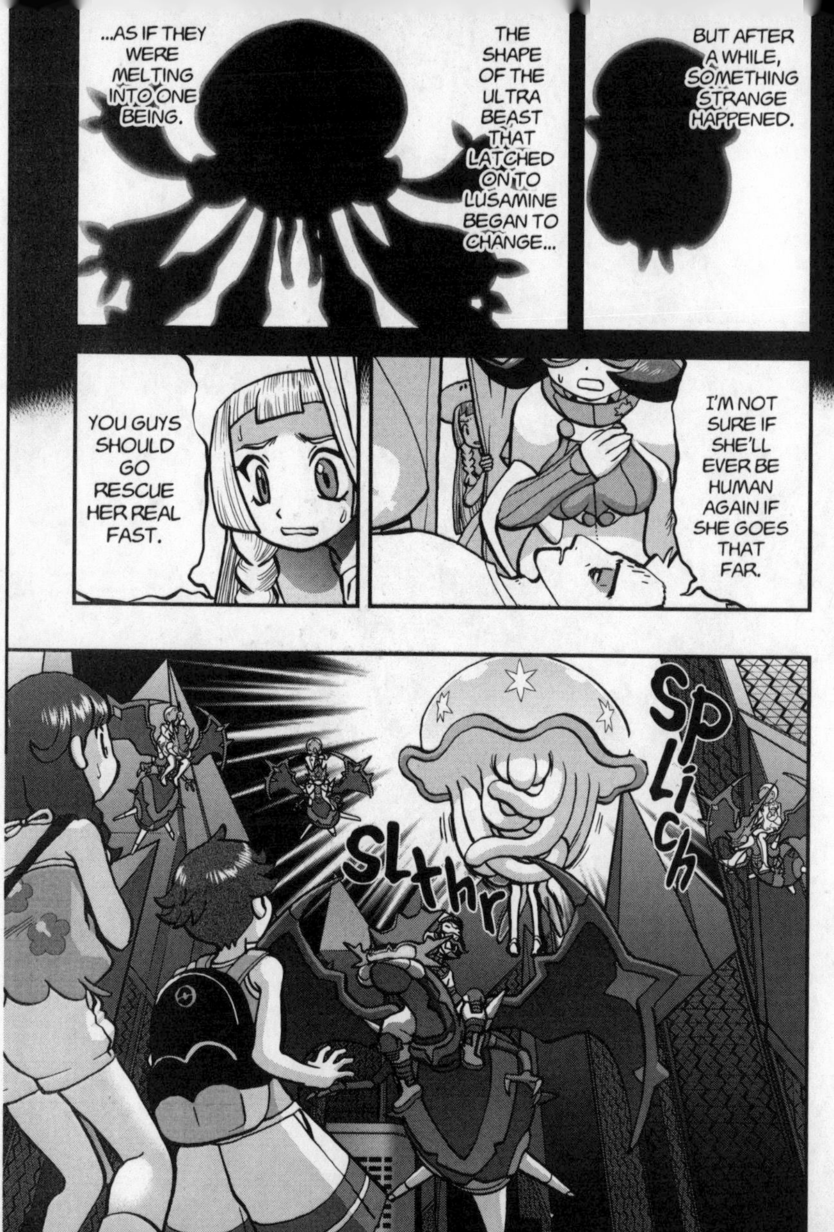
BUT AFTER A WHILE, SOMETHING STRANGE HAPPENED.
THE SHAPE OF THE ULTRA BEAST THAT LATCHED ON TO LUSAMINE BEGAN TO CHANGE...
...AS IF THEY WERE MELTING INTO ONE BEING.
I'M NOT SURE IF SHE'LL EVER BE HUMAN AGAIN IF SHE GOES THAT FAR.
YOU GUYS SHOULD GO RESCUE HER REAL FAST.
SPLiCH
SLTHR

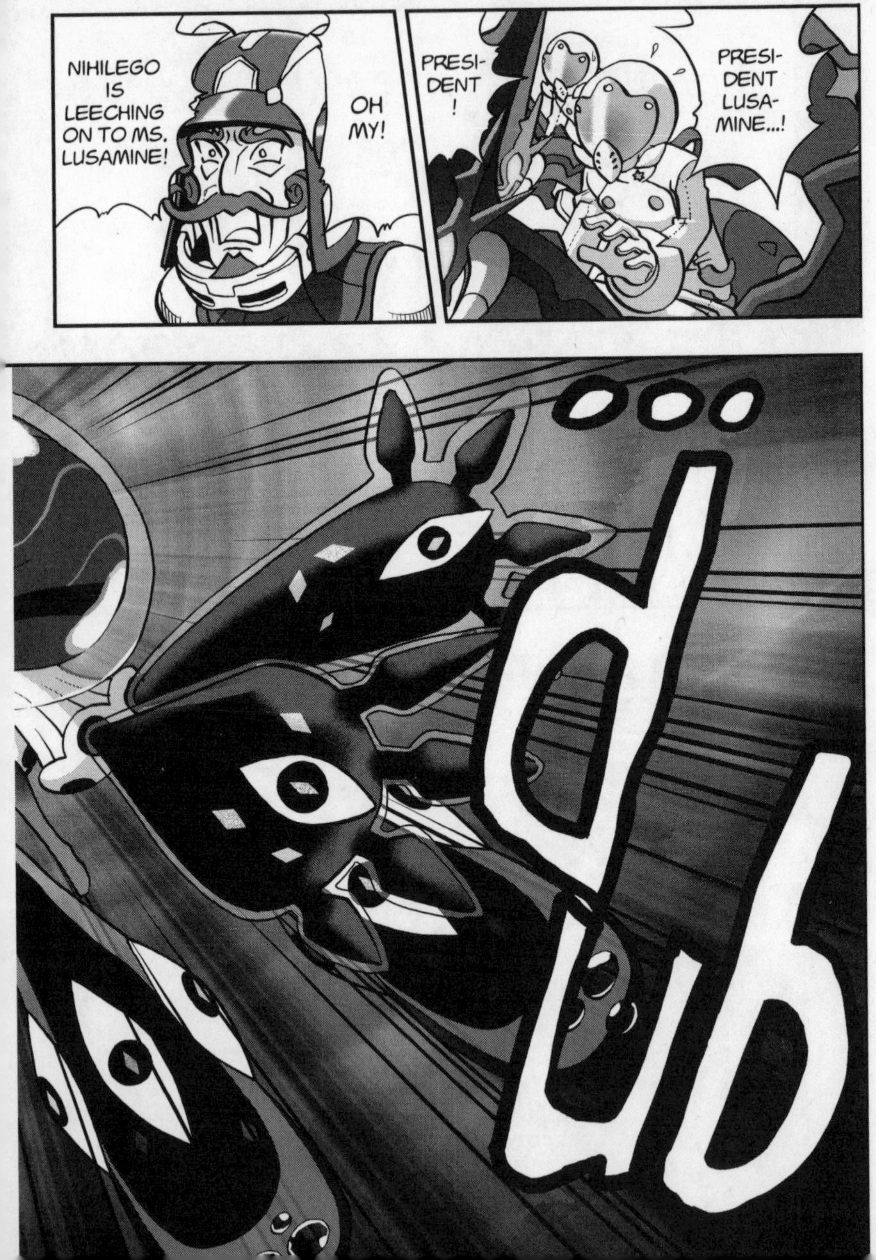
PRESI-DENT LUSA-MINE...!
PRESI-DENT !
OH MY!
NIHILEGO IS LEECHING ON TO MS. LUSAMINE!

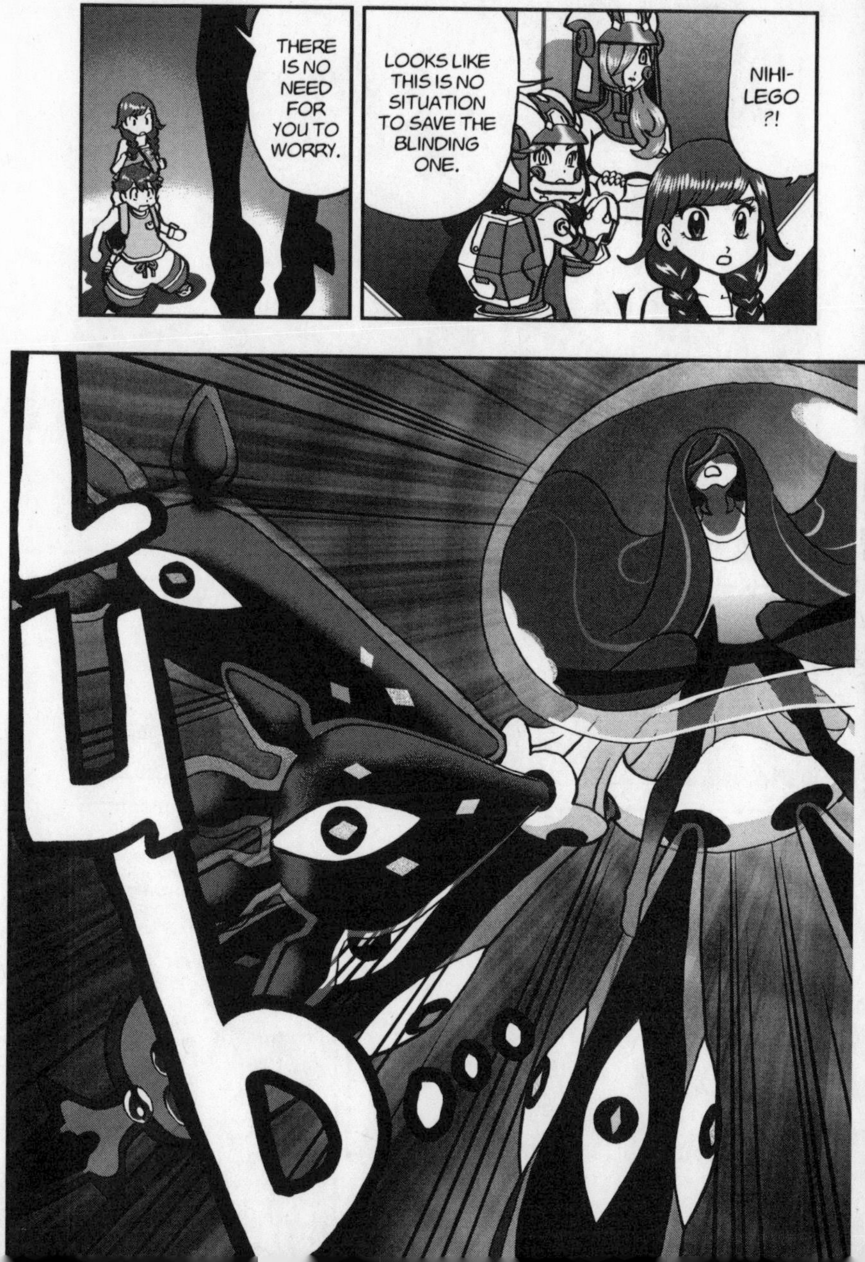
NIHI-LEGO ?!
LOOKS LIKE THIS IS NO SITUATION TO SAVE THE BLINDING ONE.
THERE IS NO NEED FOR YOU TO WORRY.

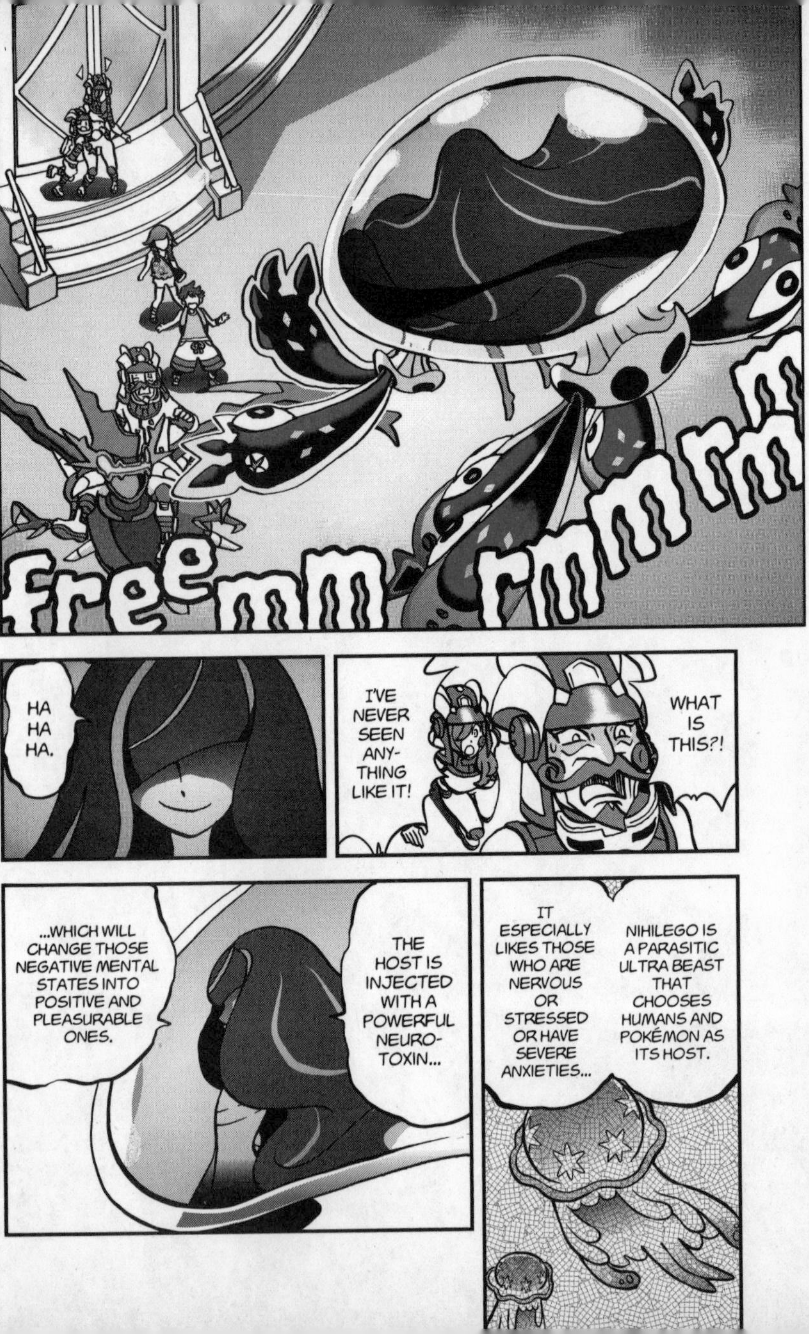
freemm
rmmrmm
WHAT IS THIS?!
I'VE NEVER SEEN ANY-THING LIKE IT!
HA HA HA.
NIHILEGO IS A PARASITIC ULTRA BEAST THAT CHOOSES HUMANS AND POKÉMON AS ITS HOST.
IT ESPECIALLY LIKES THOSE WHO ARE NERVOUS OR STRESSED OR HAVE SEVERE ANXIETIES...
THE HOST IS INJECTED WITH A POWERFUL NEURO-TOXIN...
...WHICH WILL CHANGE THOSE NEGATIVE MENTAL STATES INTO POSITIVE AND PLEASURABLE ONES.

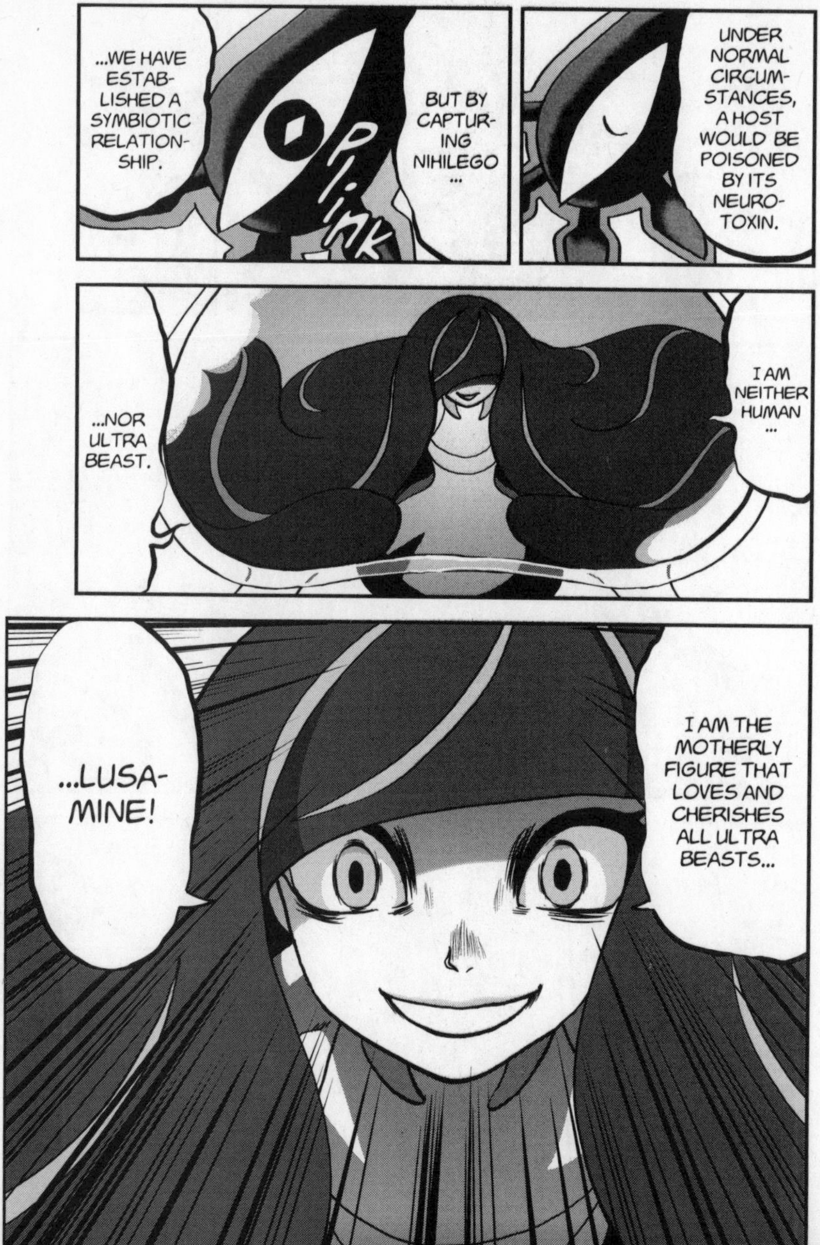
UNDER NORMAL CIRCUM-STANCES, A HOST WOULD BE POISONED BY ITS NEURO-TOXIN.
BUT BY CAPTUR-ING NIHILEGO ...
...WE HAVE ESTAB-LISHED A SYMBIOTIC RELATION-SHIP.
Plink
I AM NEITHER HUMAN ...
...NOR ULTRA BEAST.
I AM THE MOTHERLY FIGURE THAT LOVES AND CHERISHES ALL ULTRA BEASTS...
...LUSA-MINE!

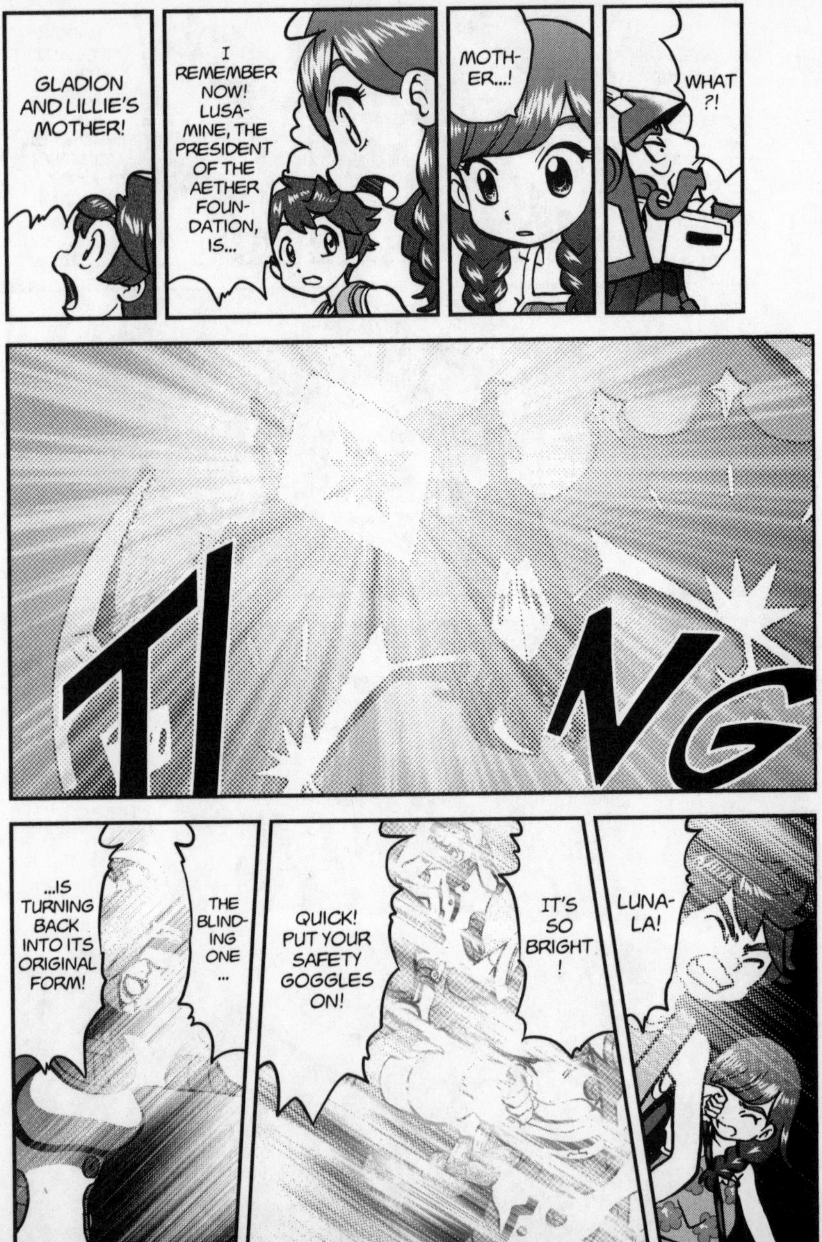
WHAT?!
MOTHER...!
I REMEMBER NOW! LUSAMINE, THE PRESIDENT OF THE AETHER FOUNDATION, IS...
GLADION AND LILLIE'S MOTHER!
TING
LUNALA!
IT'S SO BRIGHT!
QUICK! PUT YOUR SAFETY GOGGLES ON!
THE BLINDING ONE...
...IS TURNING BACK INTO ITS ORIGINAL FORM!

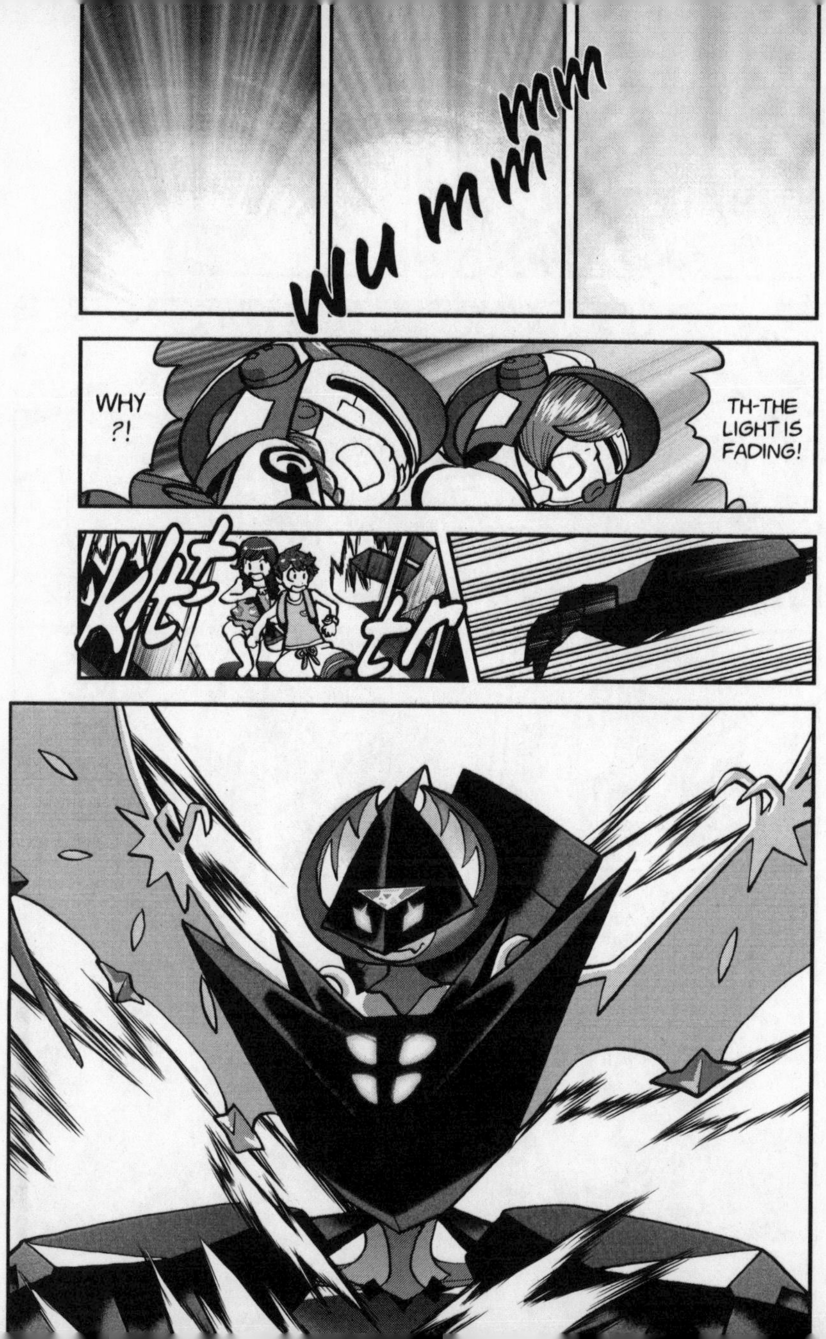
wummmmm
TH-THE LIGHT IS FADING!
WHY ?!
ktt tr

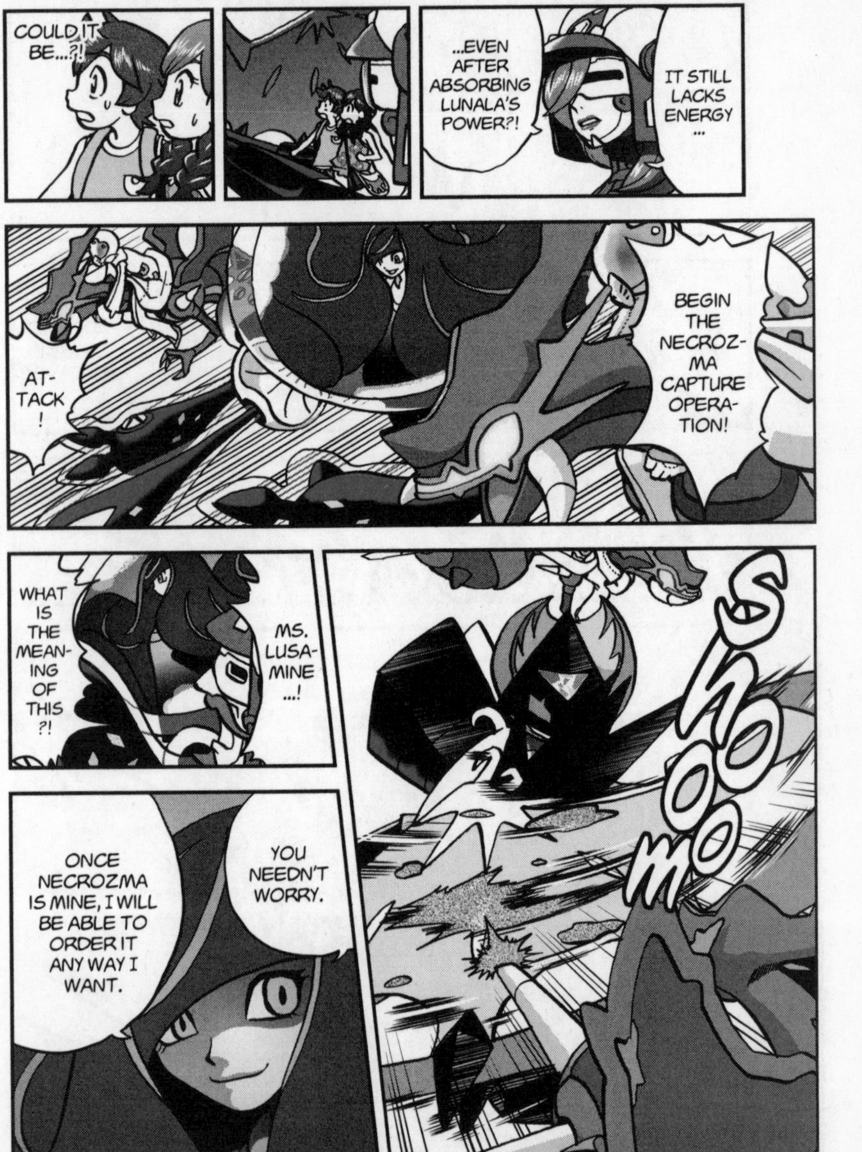
IT STILL LACKS ENERGY ...
...EVEN AFTER ABSORBING LUNALA'S POWER?!
COULD IT BE...?!
BEGIN THE NECROZMA CAPTURE OPERATION!
AT-TACK!
SHOOOOM
MS. LUSAMINE ...!
WHAT IS THE MEANING OF THIS?!
YOU NEEDN'T WORRY.
ONCE NECROZMA IS MINE, I WILL BE ABLE TO ORDER IT ANY WAY I WANT.

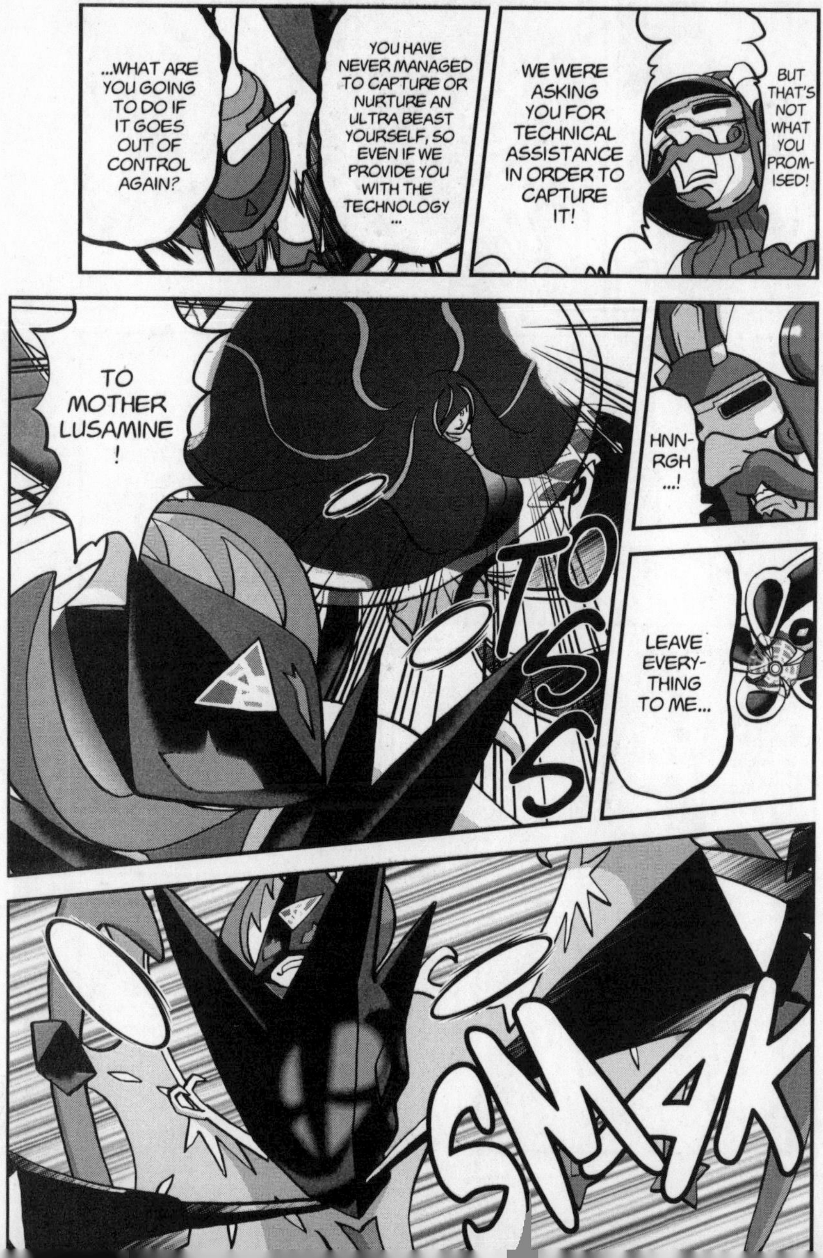
BUT THAT'S NOT WHAT YOU PROMISED!
WE WERE ASKING YOU FOR TECHNICAL ASSISTANCE IN ORDER TO CAPTURE IT!
YOU HAVE NEVER MANAGED TO CAPTURE OR NURTURE AN ULTRA BEAST YOURSELF, SO EVEN IF WE PROVIDE YOU WITH THE TECHNOLOGY...
...WHAT ARE YOU GOING TO DO IF IT GOES OUT OF CONTROL AGAIN?
HNN-RGH...!
LEAVE EVERYTHING TO ME...
TO MOTHER LUSAMINE!
TOSS
SMAK

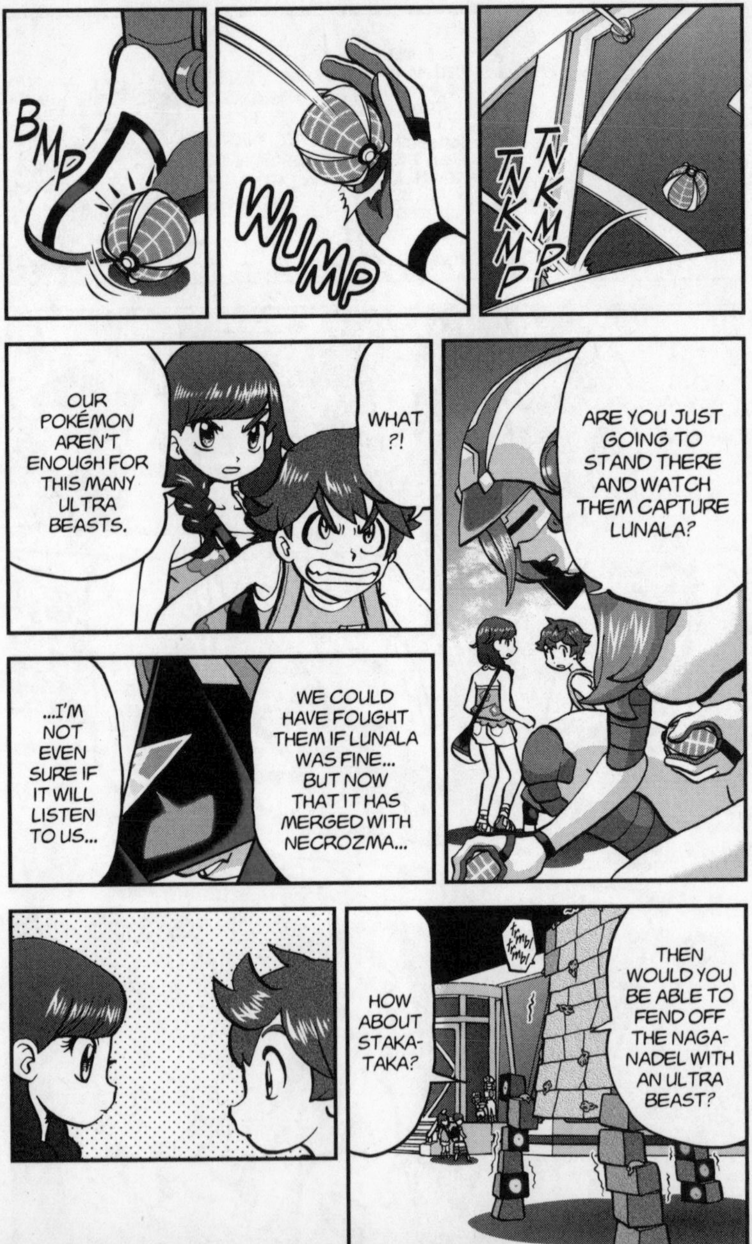
TNKMP
TNKMP
WUMP
BMP
ARE YOU JUST GOING TO STAND THERE AND WATCH THEM CAPTURE LUNALA?
WHAT?!
OUR POKÉMON AREN'T ENOUGH FOR THIS MANY ULTRA BEASTS.
WE COULD HAVE FOUGHT THEM IF LUNALA WAS FINE... BUT NOW THAT IT HAS MERGED WITH NECROZMA...
...I'M NOT EVEN SURE IF IT WILL LISTEN TO US...
THEN WOULD YOU BE ABLE TO FEND OFF THE NAGA-NADEL WITH AN ULTRA BEAST?
trmbl trmbl
HOW ABOUT STAKA-TAKA?

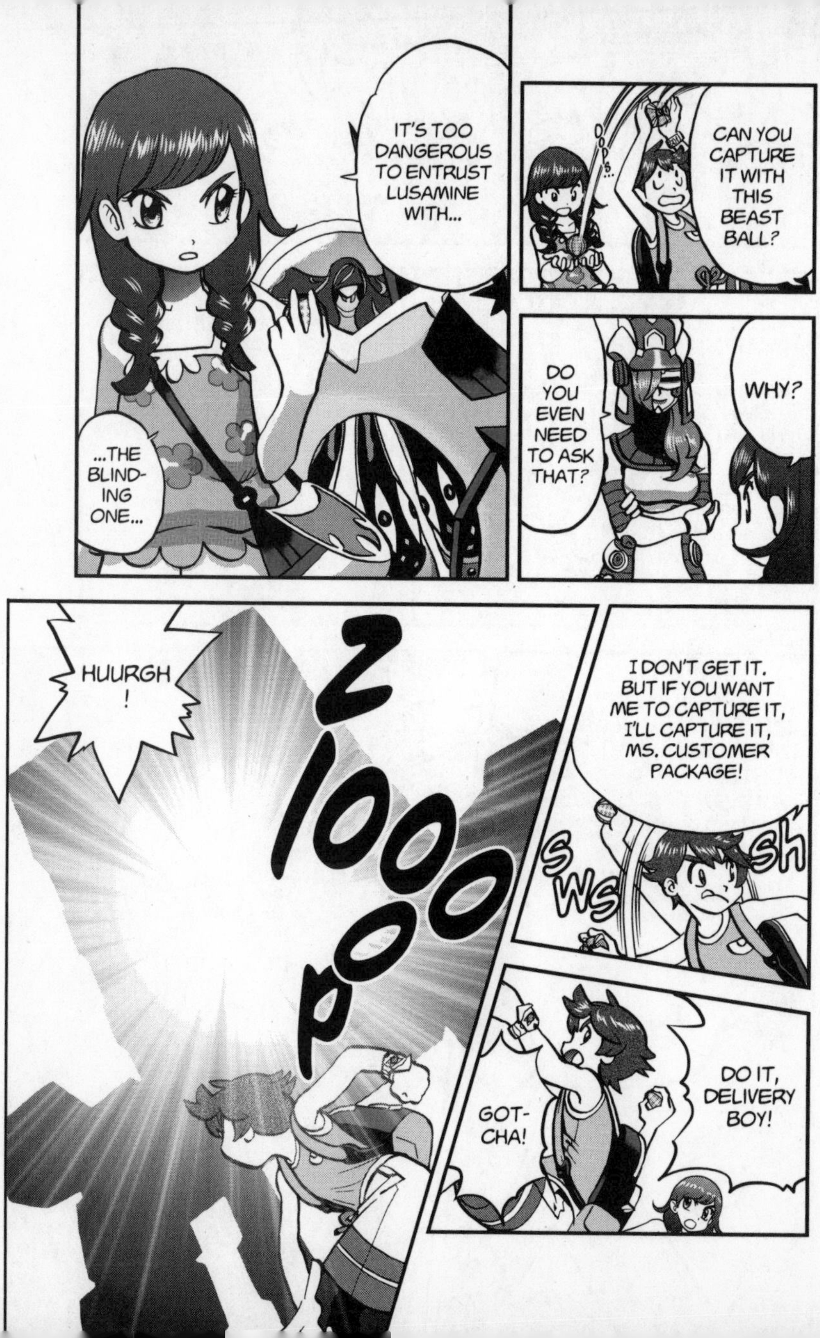
CAN YOU CAPTURE IT WITH THIS BEAST BALL?
WHY?
DO YOU EVEN NEED TO ASK THAT?
IT'S TOO DANGEROUS TO ENTRUST LUSAMINE WITH...
...THE BLIND-ING ONE...
I DON'T GET IT. BUT IF YOU WANT ME TO CAPTURE IT, I'LL CAPTURE IT, MS. CUSTOMER PACKAGE!
SWSSH
DO IT, DELIVERY BOY!
GOT-CHA!
HUURGH!
ZIOOOOOP

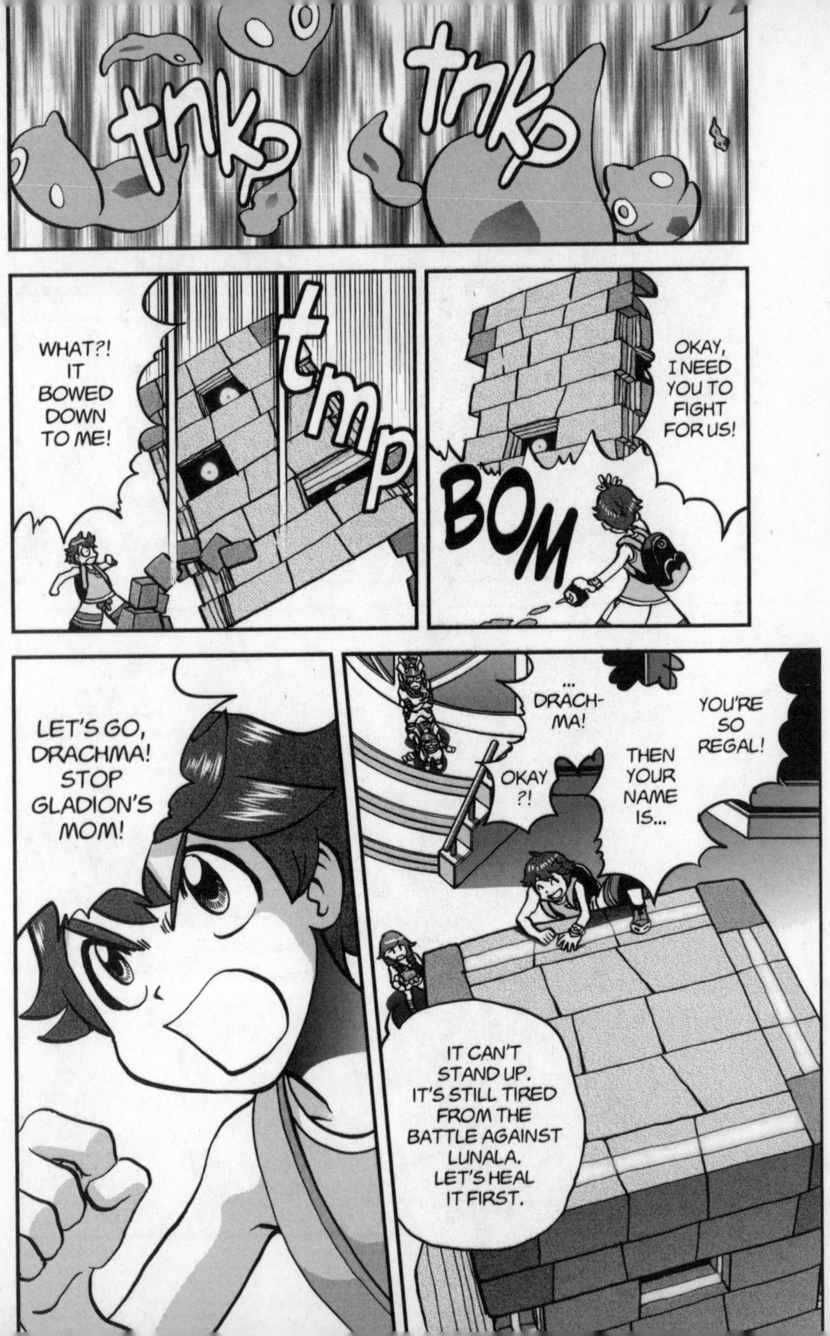
tnkp
tnkp
OKAY, I NEED YOU TO FIGHT FOR US!
BOM
WHAT?! IT BOWED DOWN TO ME!
tmp
YOU'RE SO REGAL!
THEN YOUR NAME IS...
... DRACHMA!
OKAY ?!
IT CAN'T STAND UP. IT'S STILL TIRED FROM THE BATTLE AGAINST LUNALA. LET'S HEAL IT FIRST.
LET'S GO, DRACHMA! STOP GLADION'S MOM!

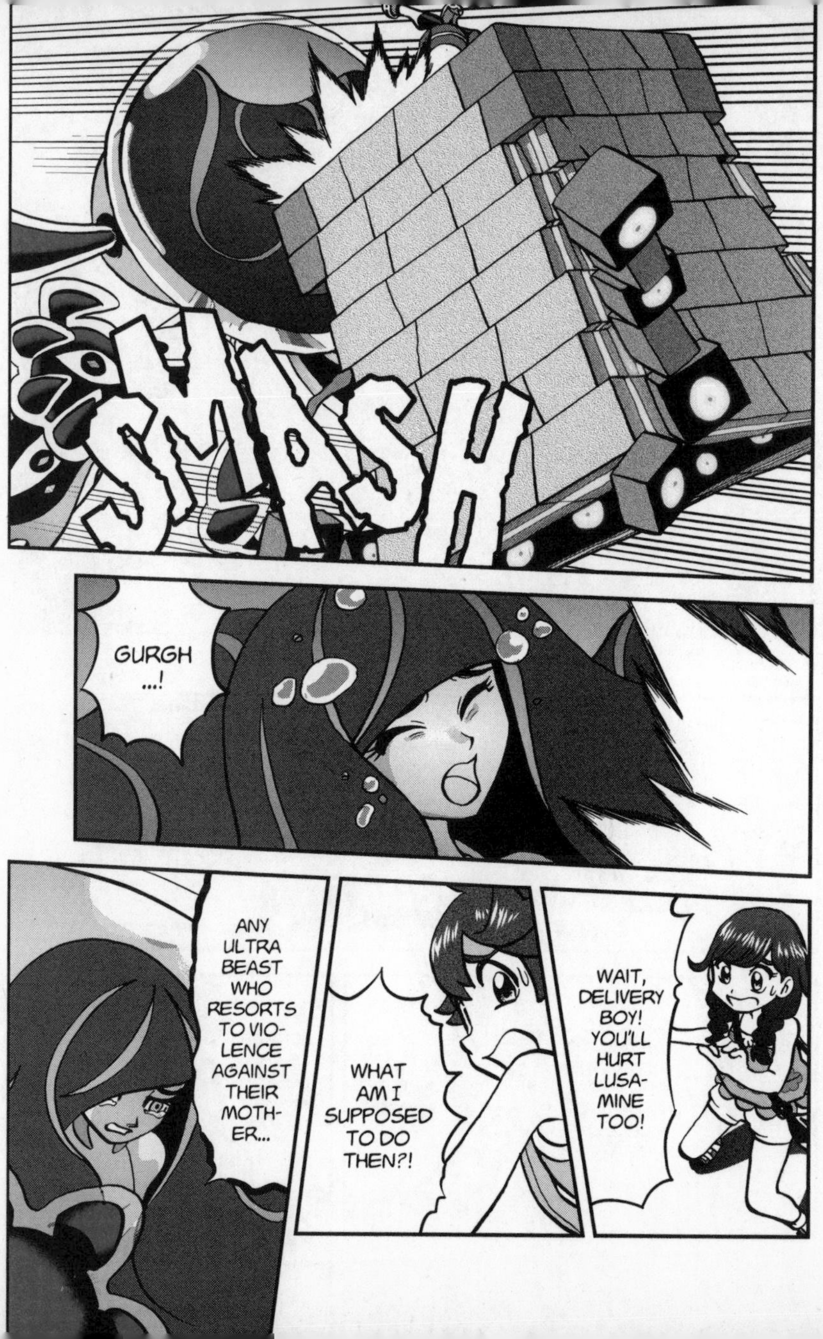
SMASH
GURGH ...!
WAIT, DELIVERY BOY! YOU'LL HURT LUSA-MINE TOO!
WHAT AM I SUPPOSED TO DO THEN?!
ANY ULTRA BEAST WHO RESORTS TO VIO-LENCE AGAINST THEIR MOTH-ER...

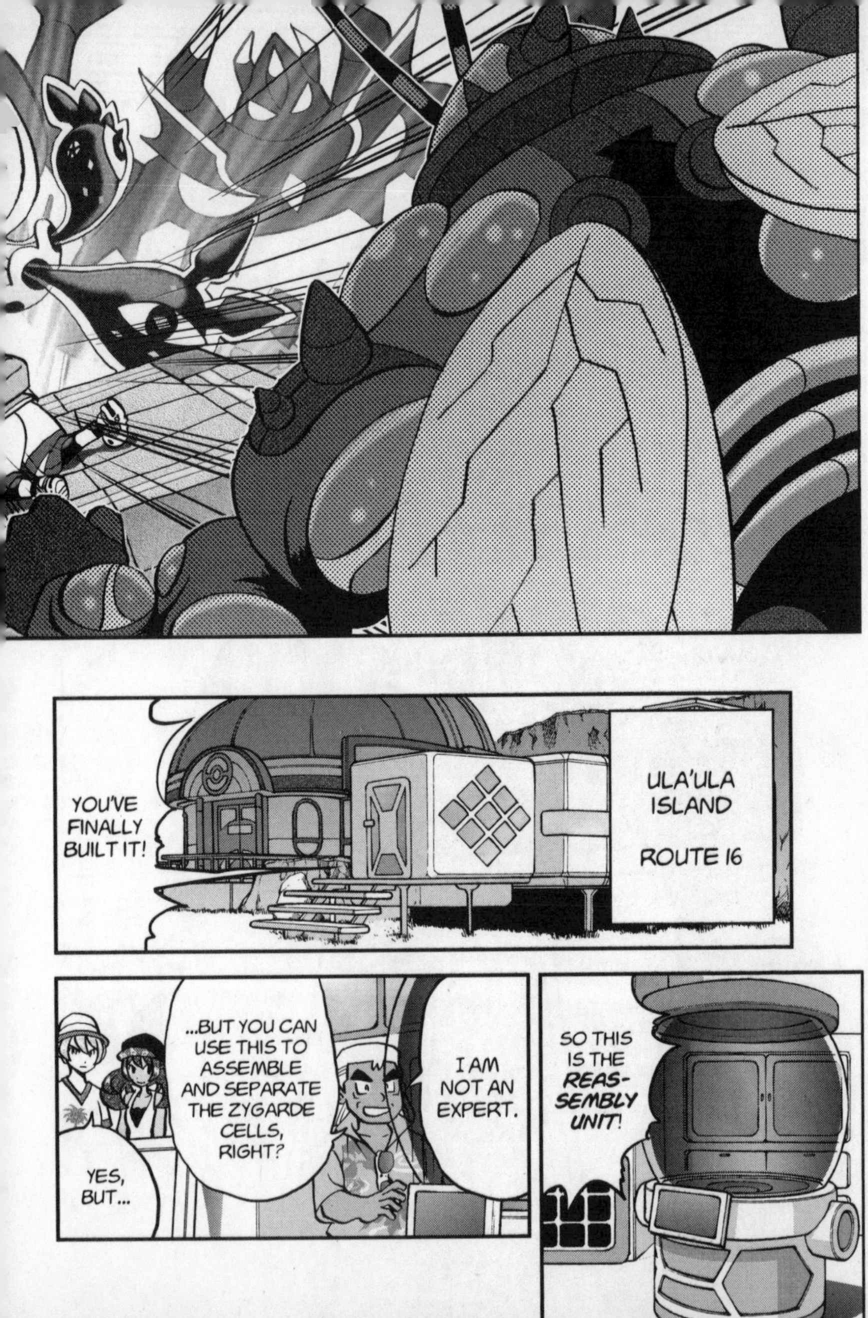
ULA'ULA ISLAND
ROUTE 16
YOU'VE FINALLY BUILT IT!
SO THIS IS THE REAS-SEMBLY UNIT!
I AM NOT AN EXPERT.
...BUT YOU CAN USE THIS TO ASSEMBLE AND SEPARATE THE ZYGARDE CELLS, RIGHT?
YES, BUT...

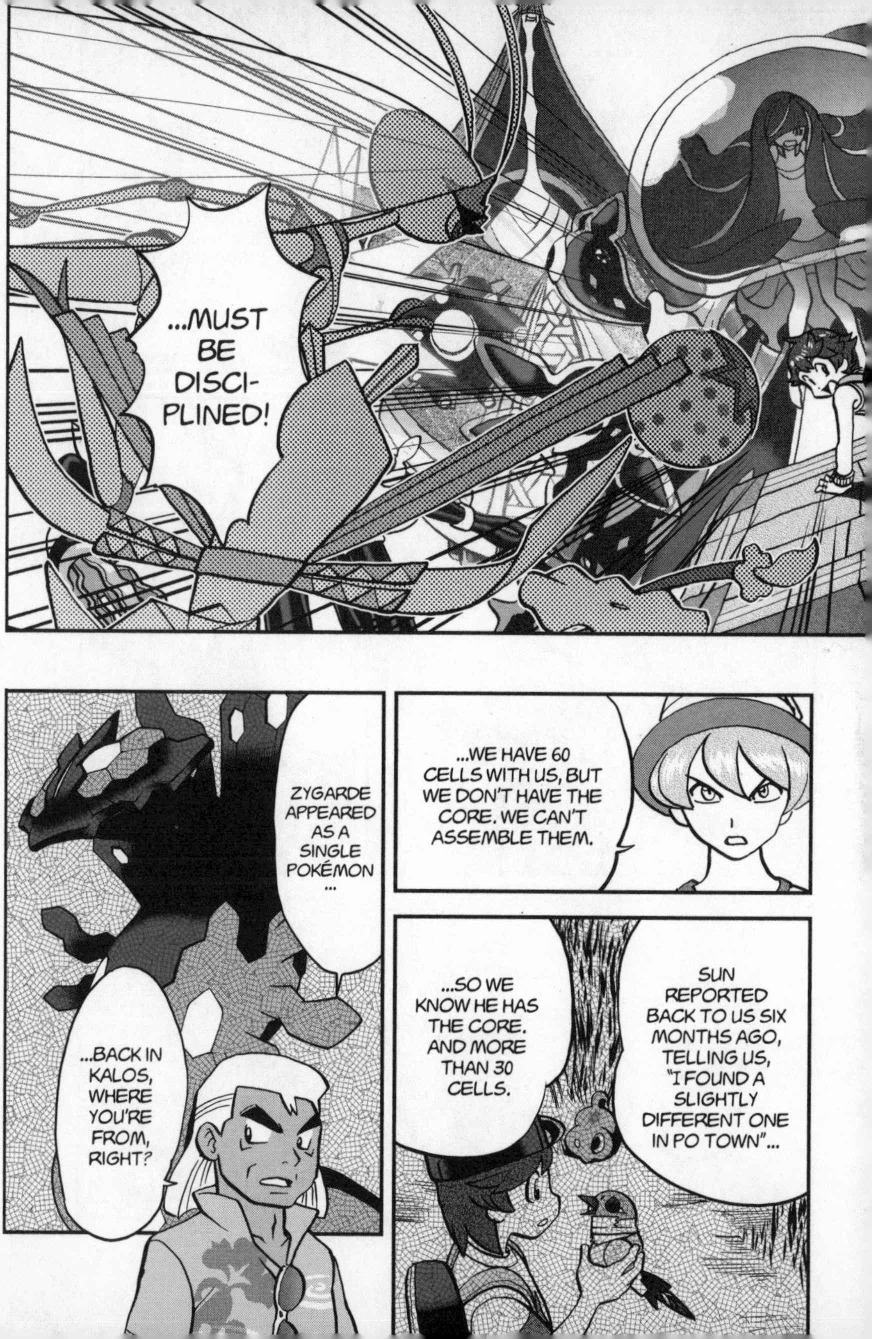
...MUST BE DISCIPLINED!
...WE HAVE 60 CELLS WITH US, BUT WE DON'T HAVE THE CORE. WE CAN'T ASSEMBLE THEM.
SUN REPORTED BACK TO US SIX MONTHS AGO, TELLING US, "I FOUND A SLIGHTLY DIFFERENT ONE IN PO TOWN"...
...SO WE KNOW HE HAS THE CORE. AND MORE THAN 30 CELLS.
ZYGARDE APPEARED AS A SINGLE POKÉMON...
...BACK IN KALOS, WHERE YOU'RE FROM, RIGHT?

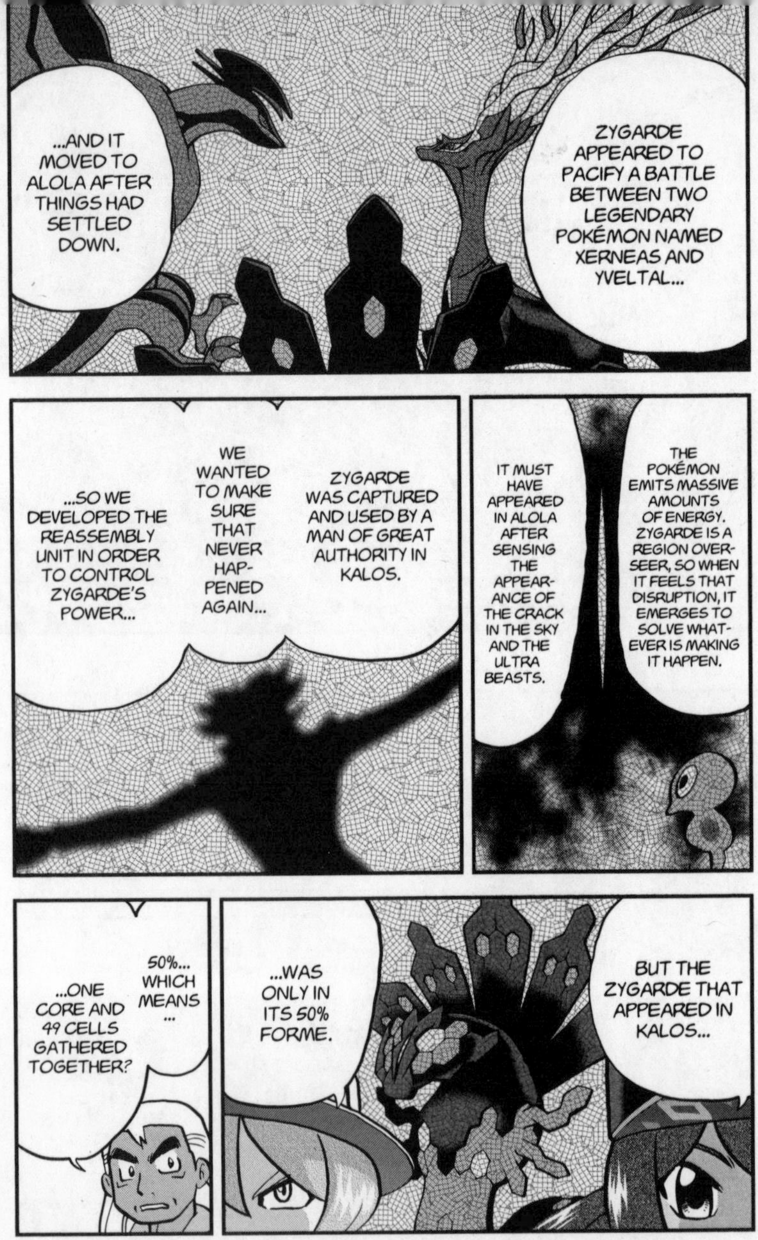
ZYGARDE APPEARED TO PACIFY A BATTLE BETWEEN TWO LEGENDARY POKÉMON NAMED XERNEAS AND YVELTAL...
...AND IT MOVED TO ALOLA AFTER THINGS HAD SETTLED DOWN.
THE POKÉMON EMITS MASSIVE AMOUNTS OF ENERGY. ZYGARDE IS A REGION OVER-SEER, SO WHEN IT FEELS THAT DISRUPTION, IT EMERGES TO SOLVE WHAT-EVER IS MAKING IT HAPPEN.
IT MUST HAVE APPEARED IN ALOLA AFTER SENSING THE APPEAR-ANCE OF THE CRACK IN THE SKY AND THE ULTRA BEASTS.
ZYGARDE WAS CAPTURED AND USED BY A MAN OF GREAT AUTHORITY IN KALOS.
WE WANTED TO MAKE SURE THAT NEVER HAP-PENED AGAIN...
...SO WE DEVELOPED THE REASSEMBLY UNIT IN ORDER TO CONTROL ZYGARDE'S POWER...
BUT THE ZYGARDE THAT APPEARED IN KALOS...
...WAS ONLY IN ITS 50% FORME.
50%... WHICH MEANS ...
...ONE CORE AND 49 CELLS GATHERED TOGETHER?

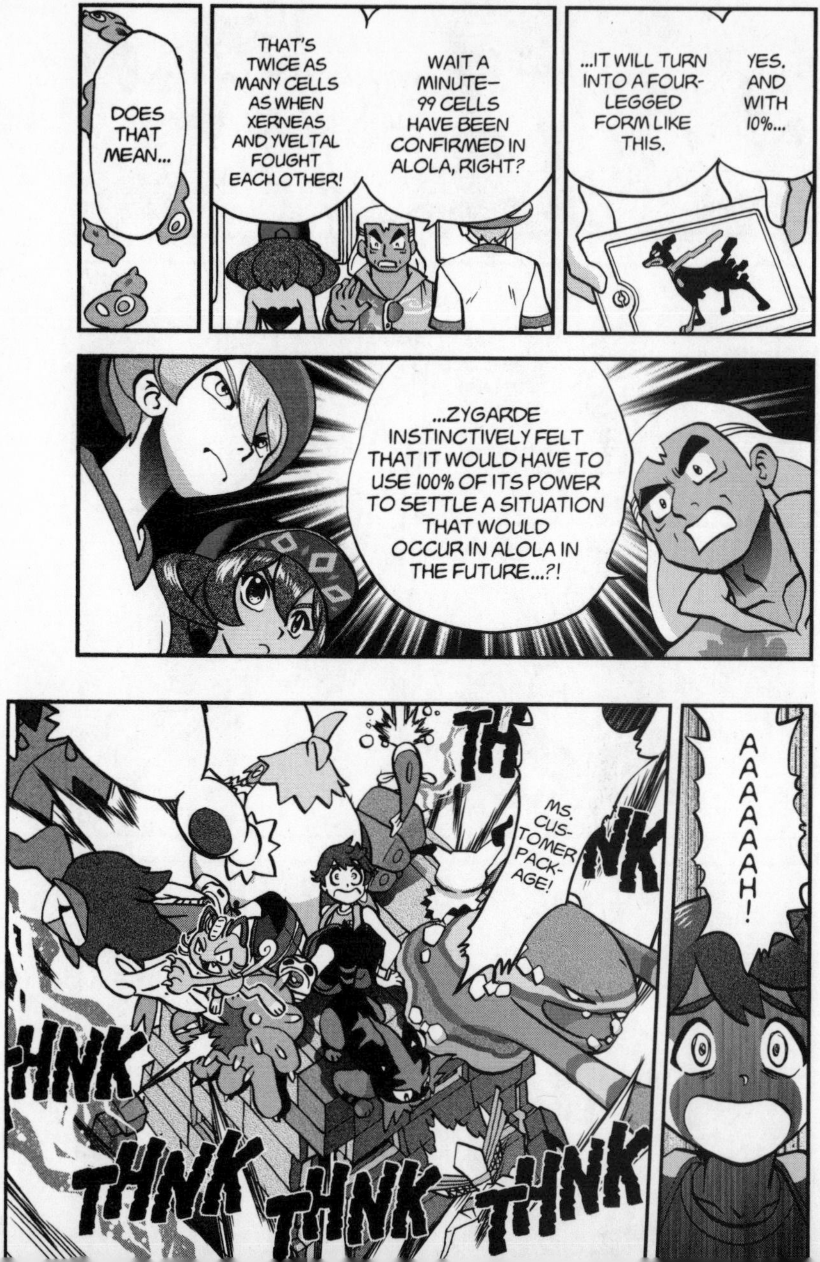
YES. AND WITH 10%...
...IT WILL TURN INTO A FOUR-LEGGED FORM LIKE THIS.
WAIT A MINUTE— 99 CELLS HAVE BEEN CONFIRMED IN ALOLA, RIGHT?
THAT'S TWICE AS MANY CELLS AS WHEN XERNEAS AND YVELTAL FOUGHT EACH OTHER!
DOES THAT MEAN...
...ZYGARDE INSTINCTIVELY FELT THAT IT WOULD HAVE TO USE 100% OF ITS POWER TO SETTLE A SITUATION THAT WOULD OCCUR IN ALOLA IN THE FUTURE...?!
AAAAAAAH!
THNK
MS. CUSTOMER PACKAGE!
THNK
THNK THNK THNK

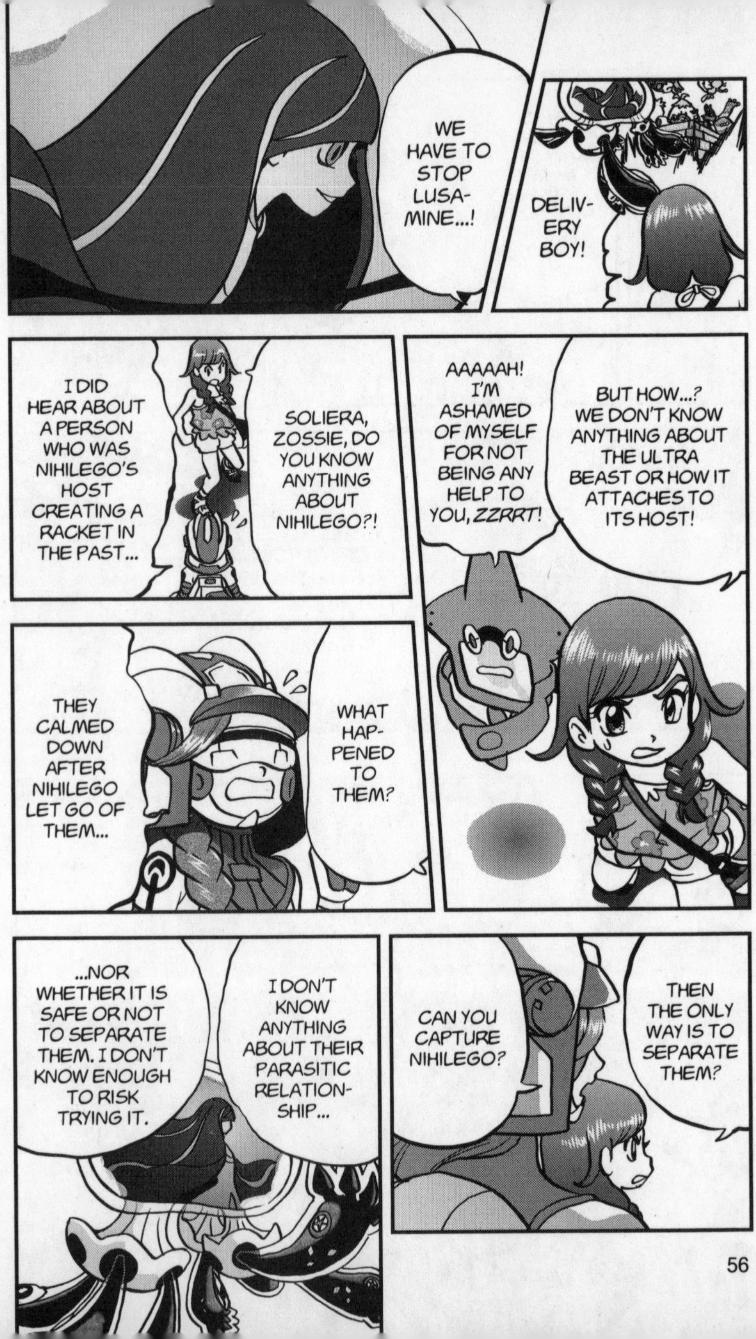
DELIV-ERY BOY!
WE HAVE TO STOP LUSA-MINE...!
BUT HOW...? WE DON'T KNOW ANYTHING ABOUT THE ULTRA BEAST OR HOW IT ATTACHES TO ITS HOST!
AAAAAH! I'M ASHAMED OF MYSELF FOR NOT BEING ANY HELP TO YOU, ZZRRT!
SOLIERA, ZOSSIE, DO YOU KNOW ANYTHING ABOUT NIHILEGO?!
I DID HEAR ABOUT A PERSON WHO WAS NIHILEGO'S HOST CREATING A RACKET IN THE PAST...
WHAT HAP-PENED TO THEM?
THEY CALMED DOWN AFTER NIHILEGO LET GO OF THEM...
THEN THE ONLY WAY IS TO SEPARATE THEM?
CAN YOU CAPTURE NIHILEGO?
I DON'T KNOW ANYTHING ABOUT THEIR PARASITIC RELATION-SHIP...
...NOR WHETHER IT IS SAFE OR NOT TO SEPARATE THEM. I DON'T KNOW ENOUGH TO RISK TRYING IT.

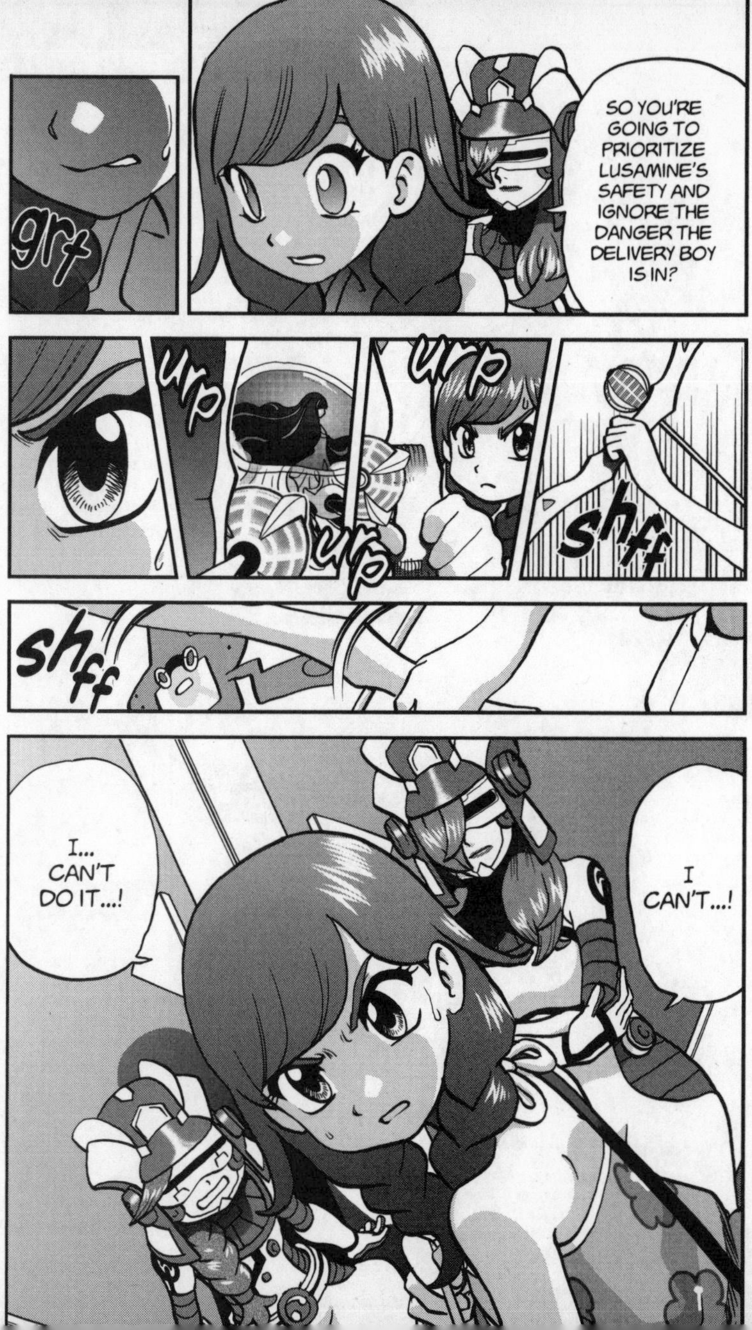
SO YOU'RE GOING TO PRIORITIZE LUSAMINE'S SAFETY AND IGNORE THE DANGER THE DELIVERY BOY IS IN?
grt
shff
urp
urp
urp
shff
I CAN'T...!
I... CAN'T DO IT...!

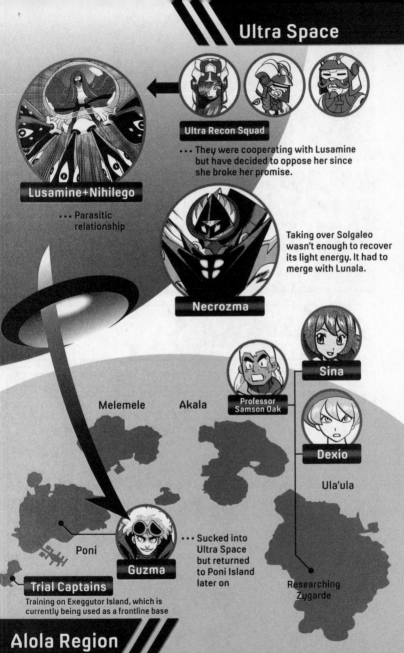

Ultra Space

Ultra Recon Squad

... They were cooperating with Lusamine but have decided to oppose her since she broke her promise.

Lusamine+Nihilego

... Parasitic relationship

Taking over Solgaleo wasn't enough to recover its light energy. It had to merge with Lunala.

Necrozma

Sina

Professor Samson Oak

Dexio

Ula'ula

Melemele   Akala

... Sucked into Ultra Space but returned to Poni Island later on

Poni

Guzma

Trial Captains

Training on Exeggutor Island, which is currently being used as a frontline base

Researching Zygarde

Alola Region

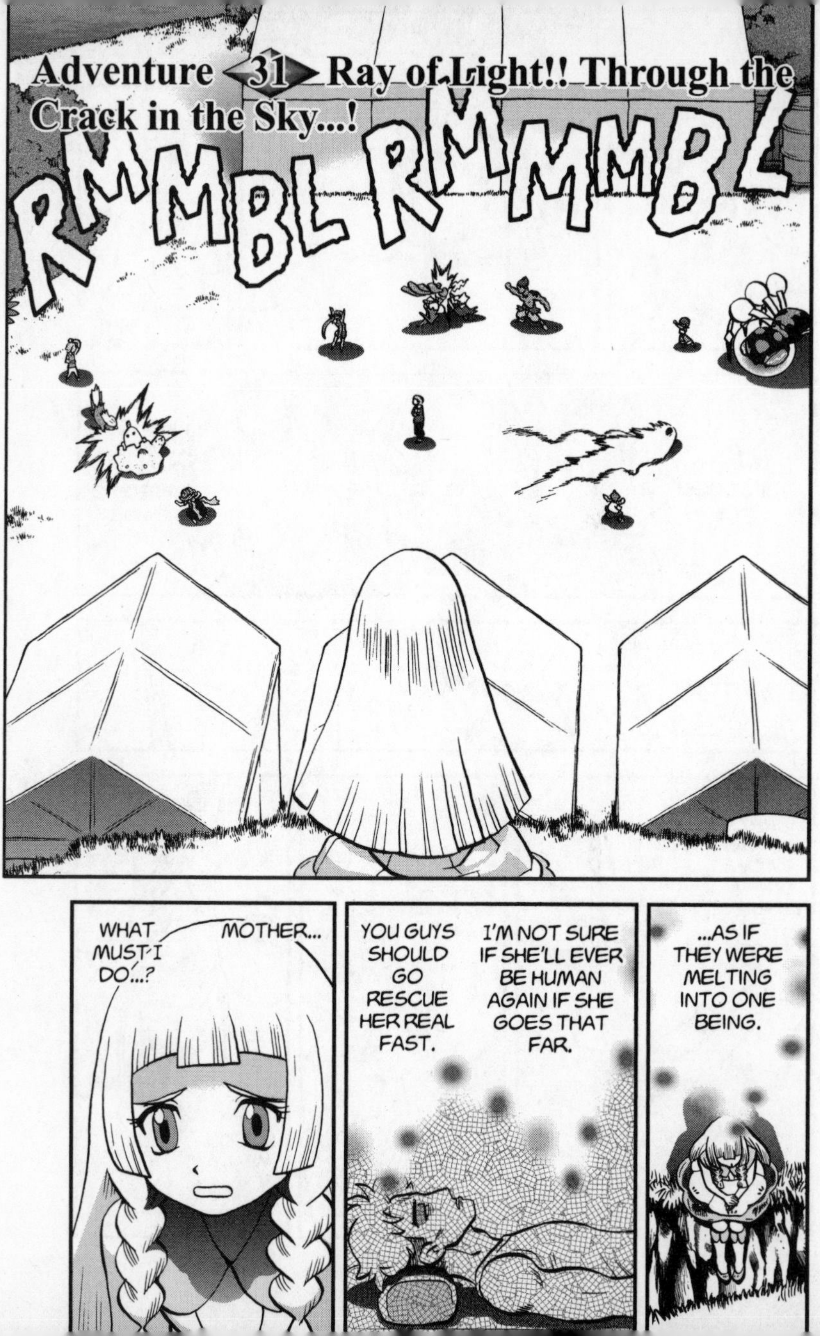
Adventure 31 Ray of Light!! Through the Crack in the Sky...!
RMMBL RMMMBL
...AS IF THEY WERE MELTING INTO ONE BEING.
I'M NOT SURE IF SHE'LL EVER BE HUMAN AGAIN IF SHE GOES THAT FAR.
YOU GUYS SHOULD GO RESCUE HER REAL FAST.
MOTHER...
WHAT MUST I DO...?

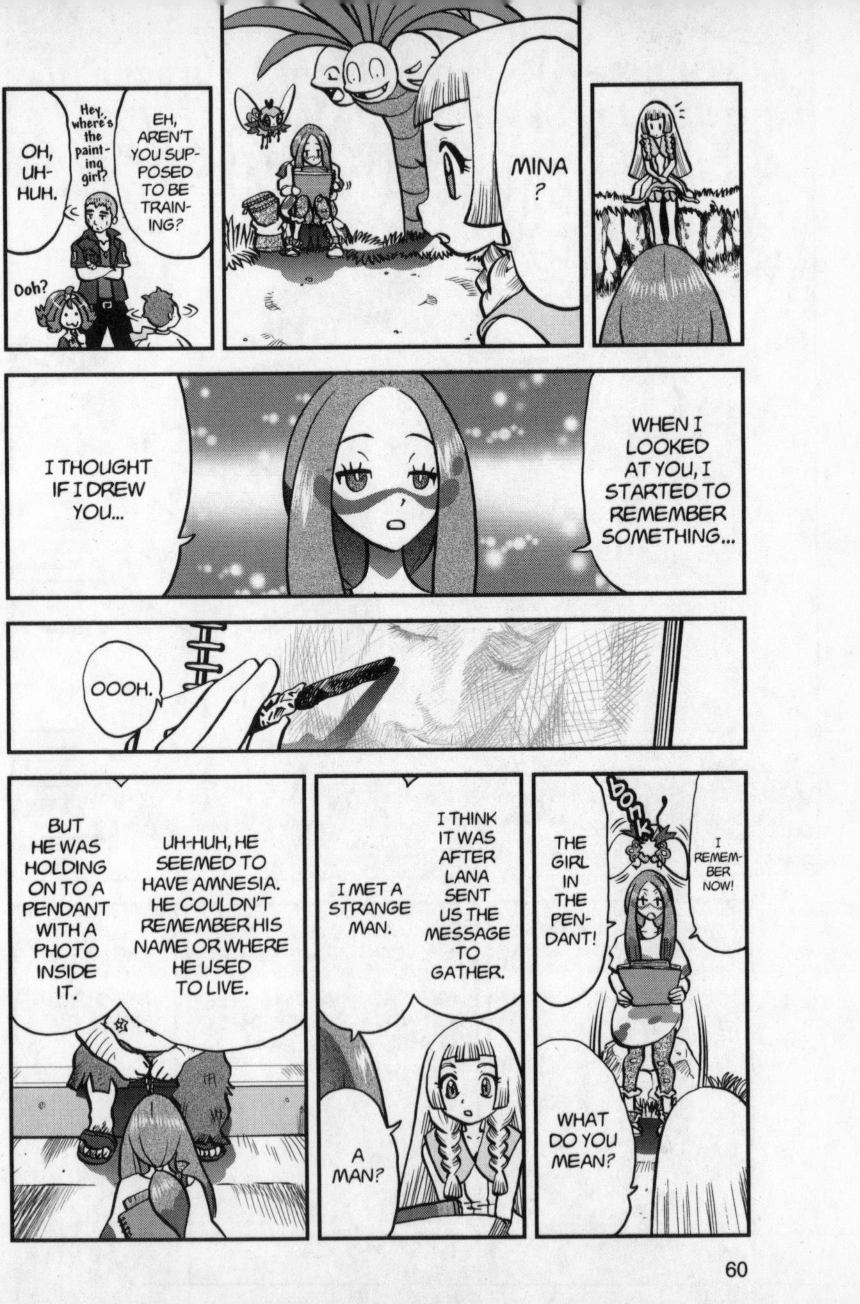
MINA?
EH, AREN'T YOU SUPPOSED TO BE TRAINING?
Hey, where's the painting girl?
OH, UH-HUH.
Ooh?
WHEN I LOOKED AT YOU, I STARTED TO REMEMBER SOMETHING...
I THOUGHT IF I DREW YOU...
OOOH.
I REMEMBER NOW!
THE GIRL IN THE PENDANT!
bonk
WHAT DO YOU MEAN?
I THINK IT WAS AFTER LANA SENT US THE MESSAGE TO GATHER.
I MET A STRANGE MAN.
A MAN?
UH-HUH, HE SEEMED TO HAVE AMNESIA. HE COULDN'T REMEMBER HIS NAME OR WHERE HE USED TO LIVE.
BUT HE WAS HOLDING ON TO A PENDANT WITH A PHOTO INSIDE IT.

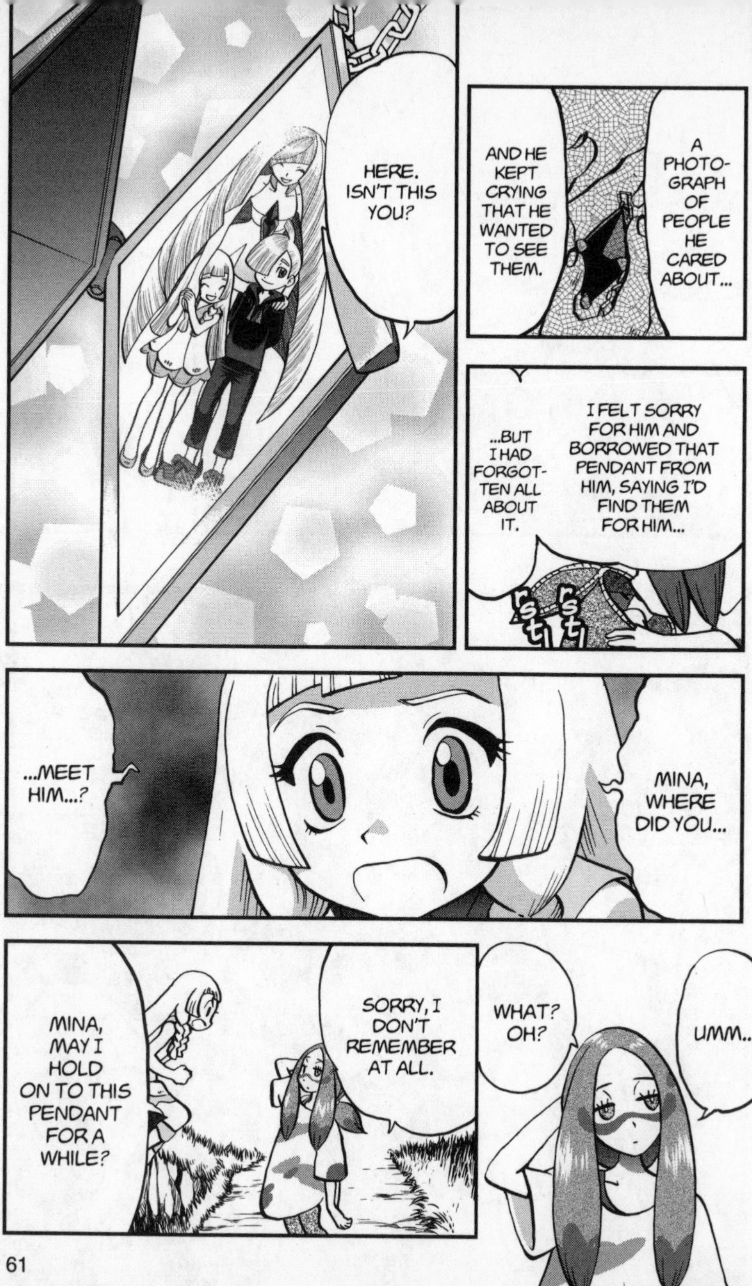
A PHOTOGRAPH OF PEOPLE HE CARED ABOUT...
AND HE KEPT CRYING THAT HE WANTED TO SEE THEM.
I FELT SORRY FOR HIM AND BORROWED THAT PENDANT FROM HIM, SAYING I'D FIND THEM FOR HIM...
...BUT I HAD FORGOTTEN ALL ABOUT IT.
rstl rstl
HERE. ISN'T THIS YOU?
MINA, WHERE DID YOU...
...MEET HIM...?
UMM...
WHAT? OH?
SORRY, I DON'T REMEMBER AT ALL.
MINA, MAY I HOLD ON TO THIS PENDANT FOR A WHILE?

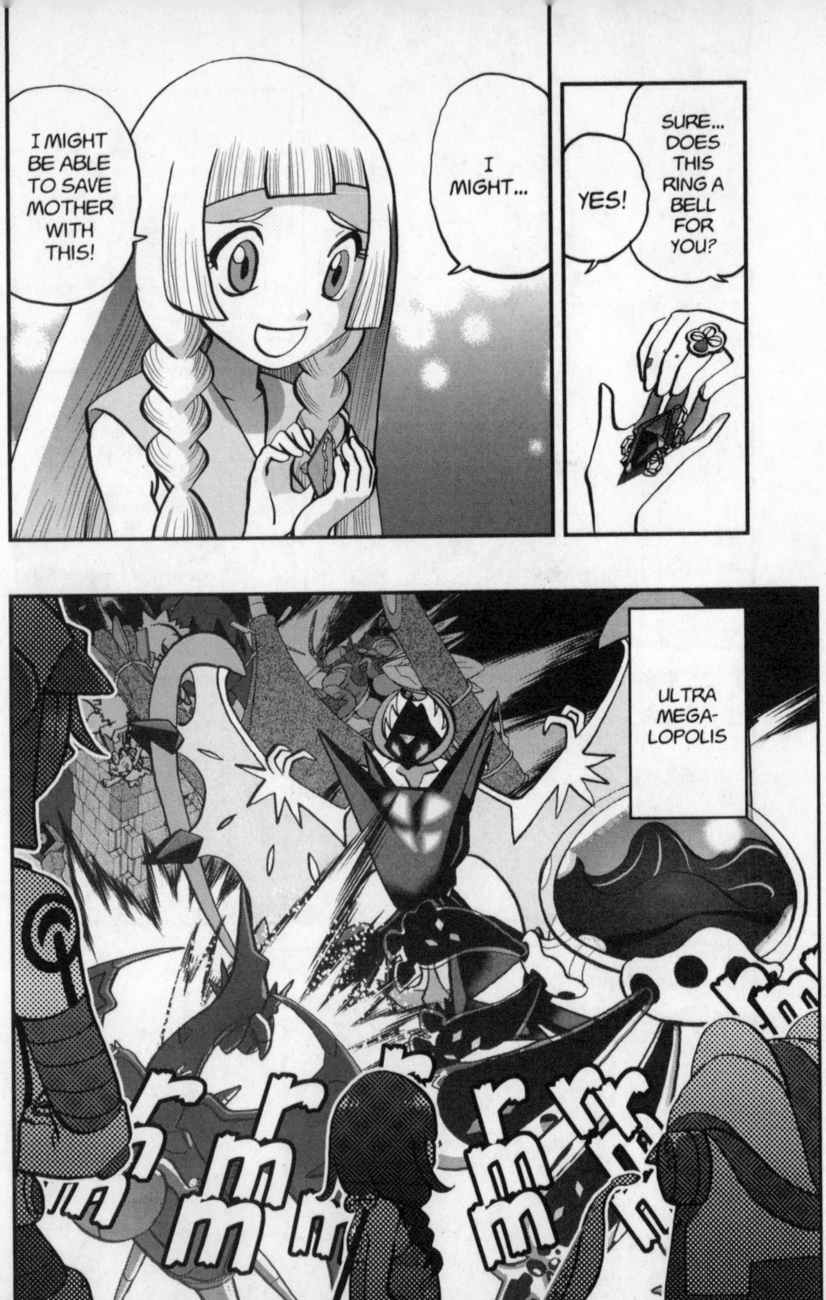
SURE... DOES THIS RING A BELL FOR YOU?
YES!
I MIGHT...
I MIGHT BE ABLE TO SAVE MOTHER WITH THIS!
ULTRA MEGA-LOPOLIS

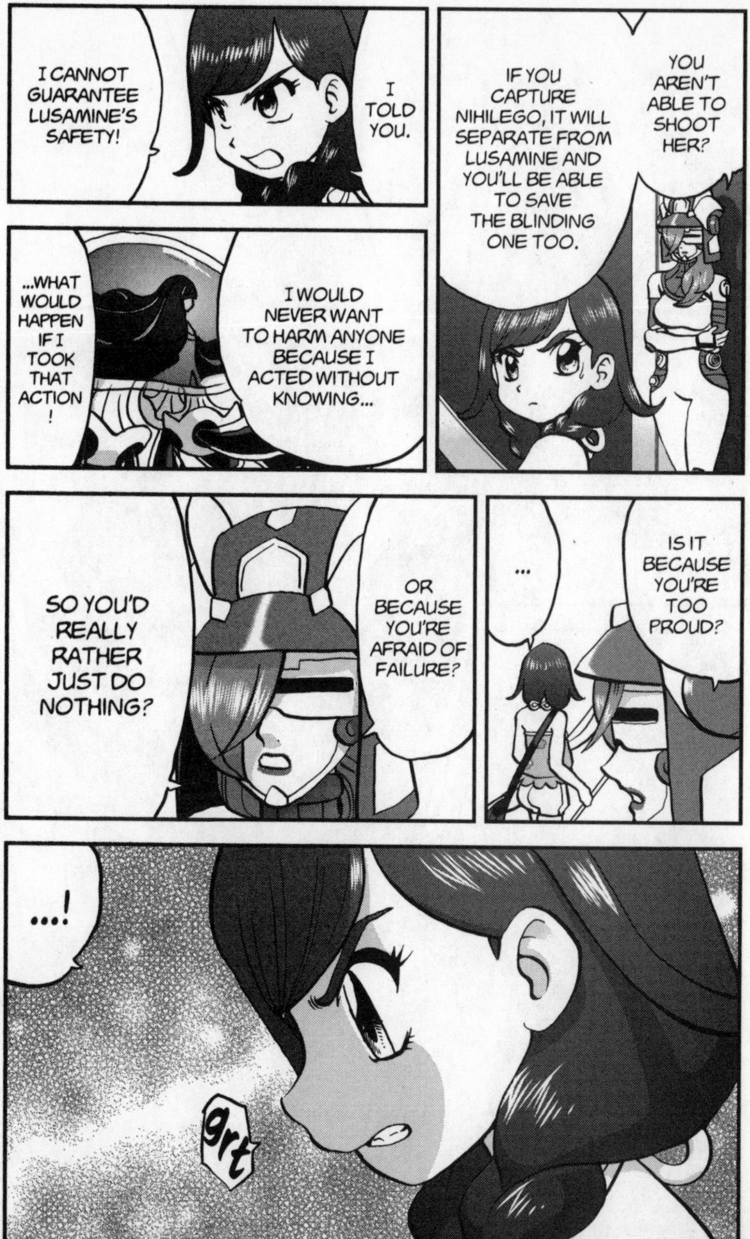
YOU AREN'T ABLE TO SHOOT HER?
IF YOU CAPTURE NIHILEGO, IT WILL SEPARATE FROM LUSAMINE AND YOU'LL BE ABLE TO SAVE THE BLINDING ONE TOO.
I TOLD YOU.
I CANNOT GUARANTEE LUSAMINE'S SAFETY!
I WOULD NEVER WANT TO HARM ANYONE BECAUSE I ACTED WITHOUT KNOWING...
...WHAT WOULD HAPPEN IF I TOOK THAT ACTION!
IS IT BECAUSE YOU'RE TOO PROUD?
...
OR BECAUSE YOU'RE AFRAID OF FAILURE?
SO YOU'D REALLY RATHER JUST DO NOTHING?
...!
grt

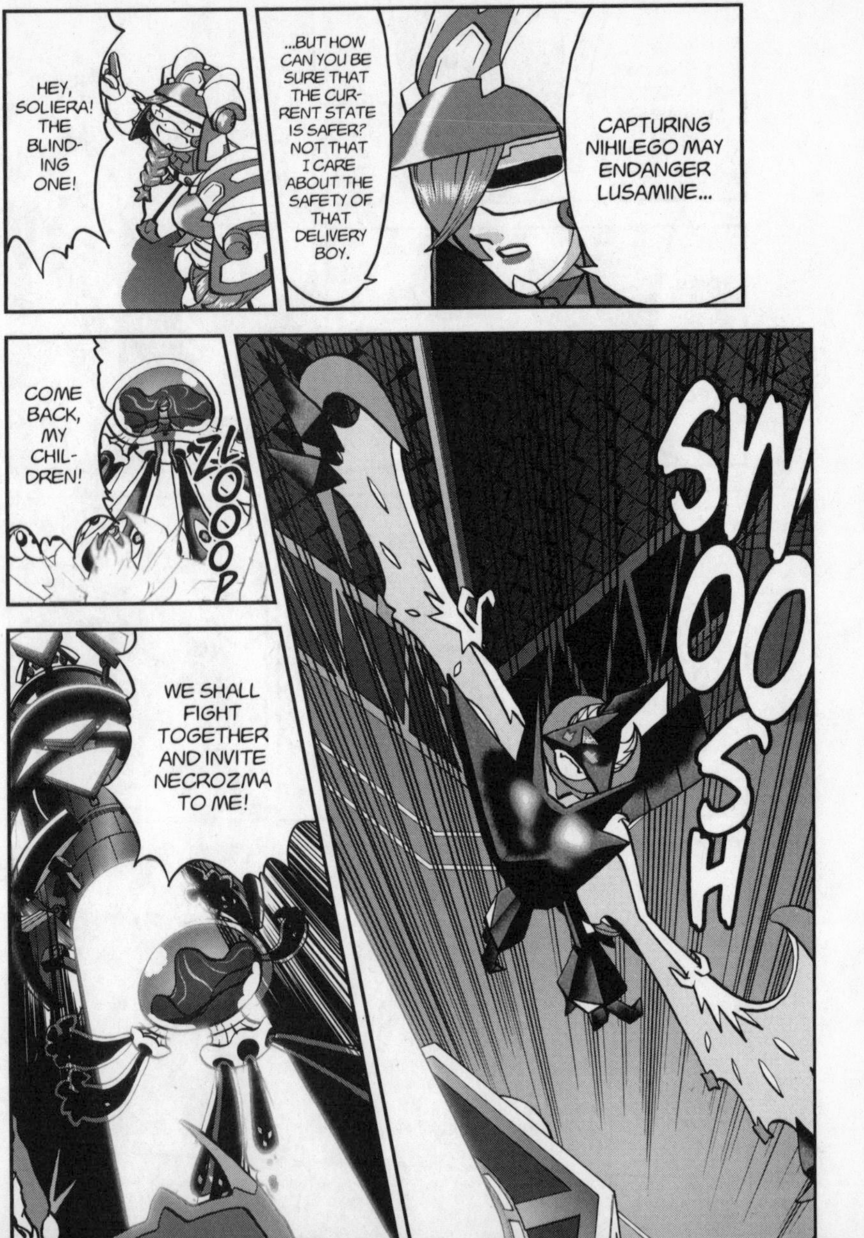
CAPTURING NIHILEGO MAY ENDANGER LUSAMINE...
...BUT HOW CAN YOU BE SURE THAT THE CUR-RENT STATE IS SAFER? NOT THAT I CARE ABOUT THE SAFETY OF THAT DELIVERY BOY.
HEY, SOLIERA! THE BLIND-ING ONE!
SWOOSH
COME BACK, MY CHIL-DREN!
ZLOOOOOP
WE SHALL FIGHT TOGETHER AND INVITE NECROZMA TO ME!

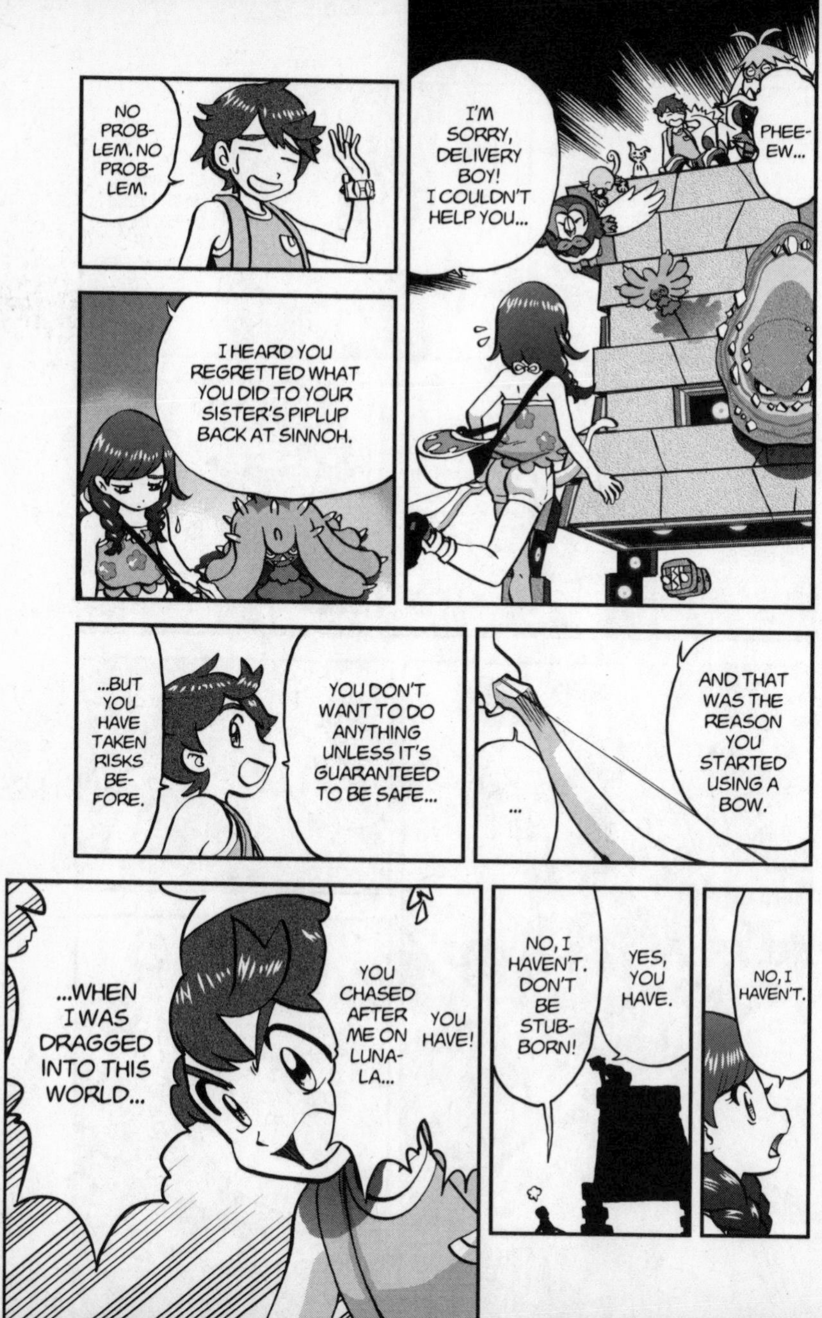
PHEEE-EW...
I'M SORRY, DELIVERY BOY! I COULDN'T HELP YOU...
NO PROBLEM. NO PROBLEM.
I HEARD YOU REGRETTED WHAT YOU DID TO YOUR SISTER'S PIPLUP BACK AT SINNOH.
AND THAT WAS THE REASON YOU STARTED USING A BOW.
...
YOU DON'T WANT TO DO ANYTHING UNLESS IT'S GUARANTEED TO BE SAFE...
...BUT YOU HAVE TAKEN RISKS BEFORE.
NO, I HAVEN'T.
YES, YOU HAVE.
NO, I HAVEN'T. DON'T BE STUBBORN!
YOU HAVE!
YOU CHASED AFTER ME ON LUNALA...
...WHEN I WAS DRAGGED INTO THIS WORLD...

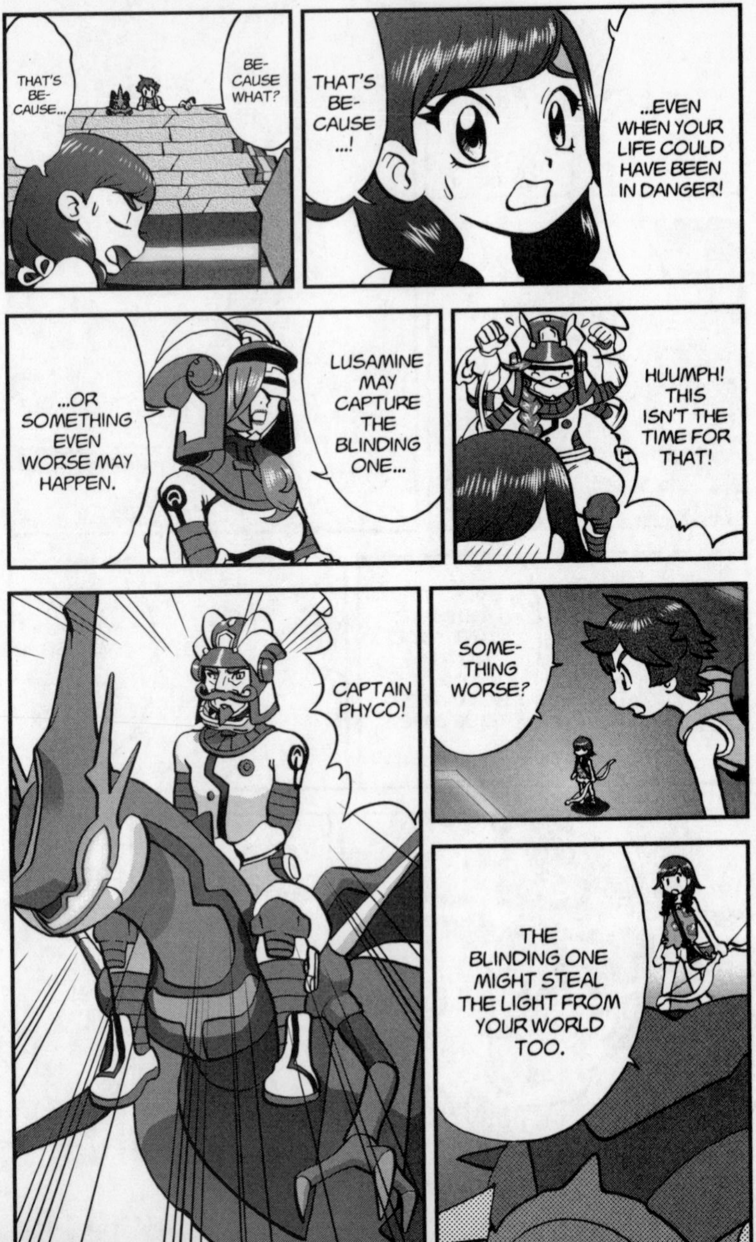
...EVEN WHEN YOUR LIFE COULD HAVE BEEN IN DANGER!
THAT'S BE-CAUSE ...!
BE-CAUSE WHAT?
THAT'S BE-CAUSE...
HUUMPH! THIS ISN'T THE TIME FOR THAT!
LUSAMINE MAY CAPTURE THE BLINDING ONE...
...OR SOMETHING EVEN WORSE MAY HAPPEN.
SOME-THING WORSE?
THE BLINDING ONE MIGHT STEAL THE LIGHT FROM YOUR WORLD TOO.
CAPTAIN PHYCO!

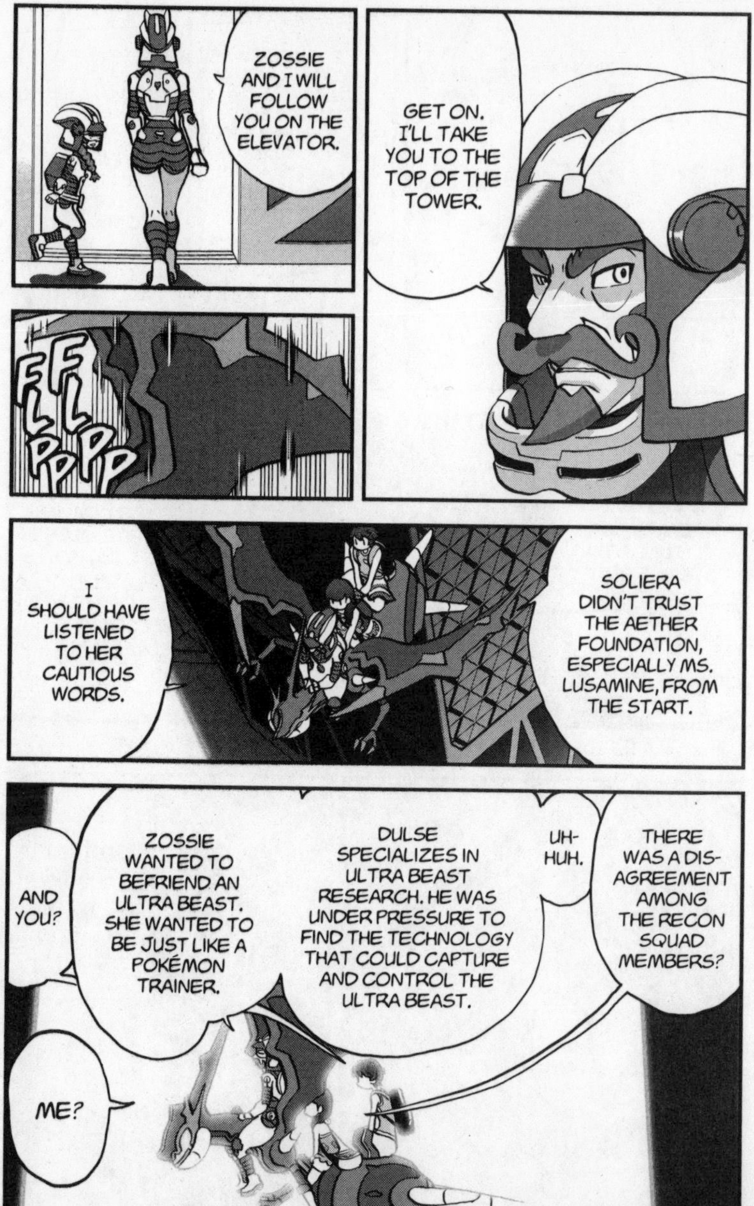
GET ON. I'LL TAKE YOU TO THE TOP OF THE TOWER.
ZOSSIE AND I WILL FOLLOW YOU ON THE ELEVATOR.
FLPP FLPP
SOLIERA DIDN'T TRUST THE AETHER FOUNDATION, ESPECIALLY MS. LUSAMINE, FROM THE START.
I SHOULD HAVE LISTENED TO HER CAUTIOUS WORDS.
THERE WAS A DIS-AGREEMENT AMONG THE RECON SQUAD MEMBERS?
UH-HUH.
DULSE SPECIALIZES IN ULTRA BEAST RESEARCH. HE WAS UNDER PRESSURE TO FIND THE TECHNOLOGY THAT COULD CAPTURE AND CONTROL THE ULTRA BEAST.
ZOSSIE WANTED TO BEFRIEND AN ULTRA BEAST. SHE WANTED TO BE JUST LIKE A POKÉMON TRAINER.
AND YOU?
ME?

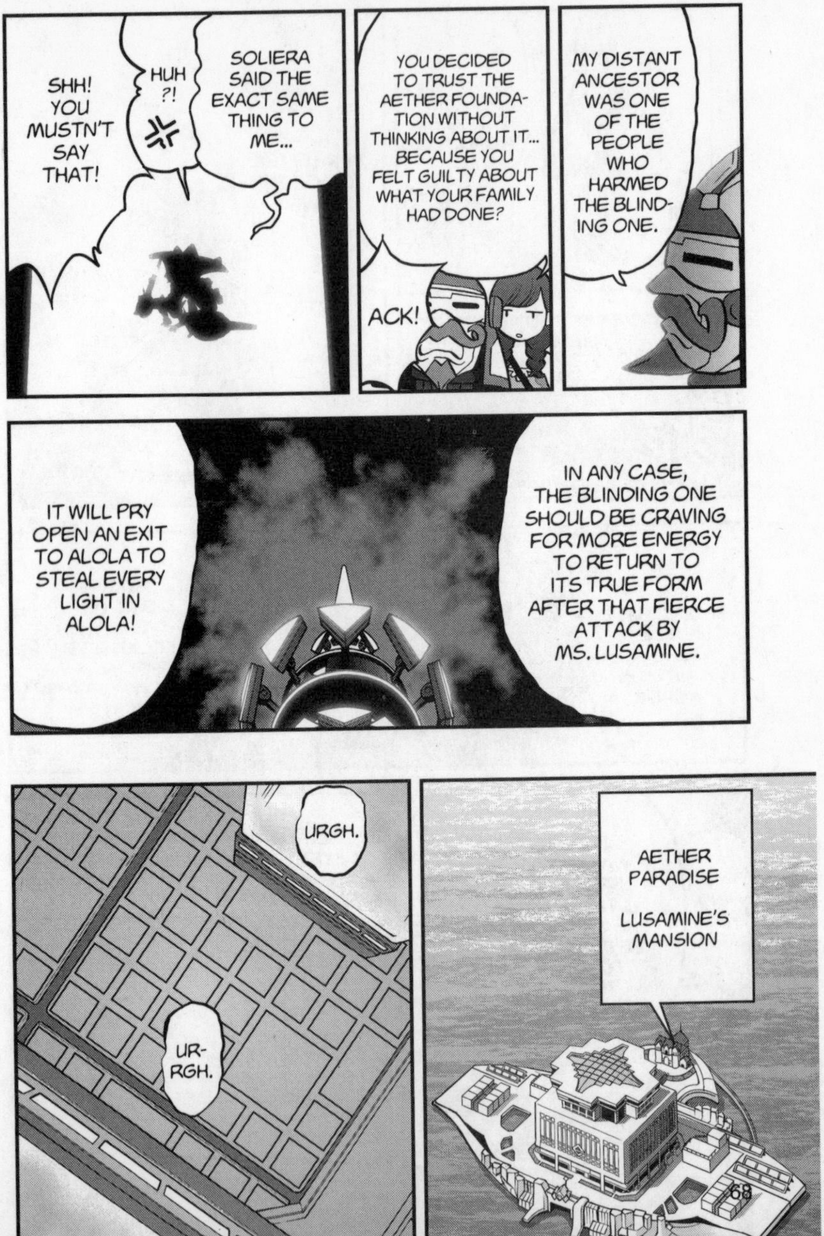
MY DISTANT ANCESTOR WAS ONE OF THE PEOPLE WHO HARMED THE BLINDING ONE.
YOU DECIDED TO TRUST THE AETHER FOUNDATION WITHOUT THINKING ABOUT IT... BECAUSE YOU FELT GUILTY ABOUT WHAT YOUR FAMILY HAD DONE?
ACK!
SOLIERA SAID THE EXACT SAME THING TO ME...
HUH ?!
SHH! YOU MUSTN'T SAY THAT!
IN ANY CASE, THE BLINDING ONE SHOULD BE CRAVING FOR MORE ENERGY TO RETURN TO ITS TRUE FORM AFTER THAT FIERCE ATTACK BY MS. LUSAMINE.
IT WILL PRY OPEN AN EXIT TO ALOLA TO STEAL EVERY LIGHT IN ALOLA!
AETHER PARADISE
LUSAMINE'S MANSION
URGH.
UR- RGH.

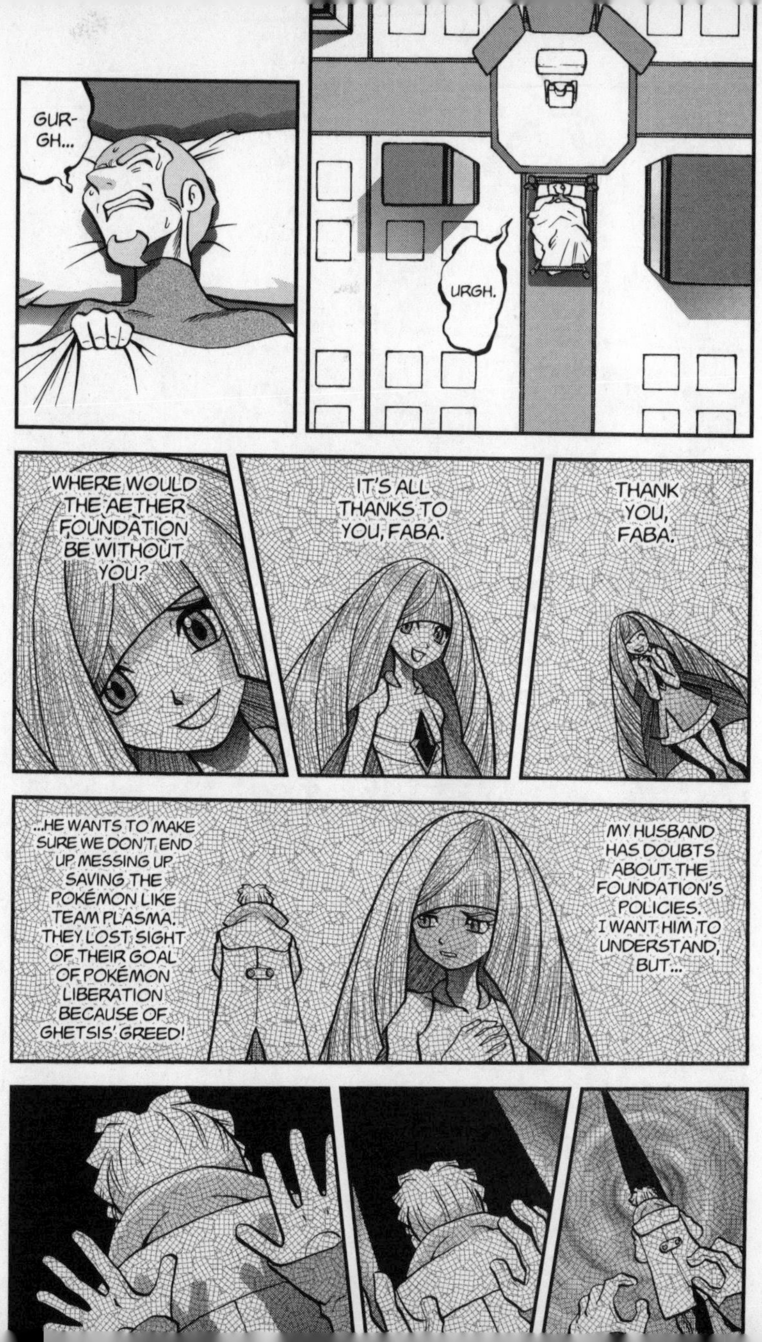
URGH.
GUR-GH...
THANK YOU, FABA.
IT'S ALL THANKS TO YOU, FABA.
WHERE WOULD THE AETHER FOUNDATION BE WITHOUT YOU?
MY HUSBAND HAS DOUBTS ABOUT THE FOUNDATION'S POLICIES. I WANT HIM TO UNDERSTAND, BUT...
...HE WANTS TO MAKE SURE WE DON'T END UP MESSING UP SAVING THE POKÉMON LIKE TEAM PLASMA. THEY LOST SIGHT OF THEIR GOAL OF POKÉMON LIBERATION BECAUSE OF GHETSIS' GREED!

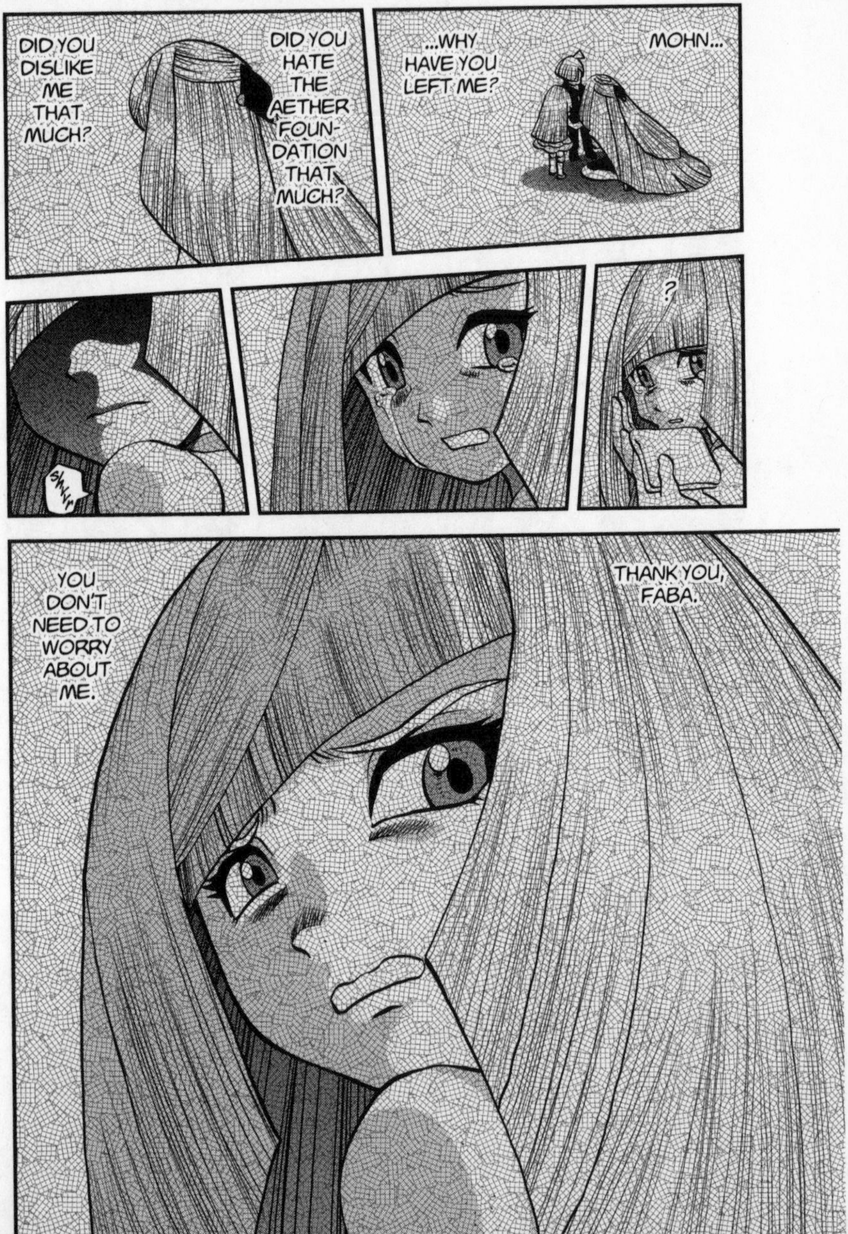
MOHN...
...WHY HAVE YOU LEFT ME?
DID YOU HATE THE AETHER FOUN-DATION THAT MUCH?
DID YOU DISLIKE ME THAT MUCH?
?
Shvvr
THANK YOU, FABA.
YOU DON'T NEED TO WORRY ABOUT ME.

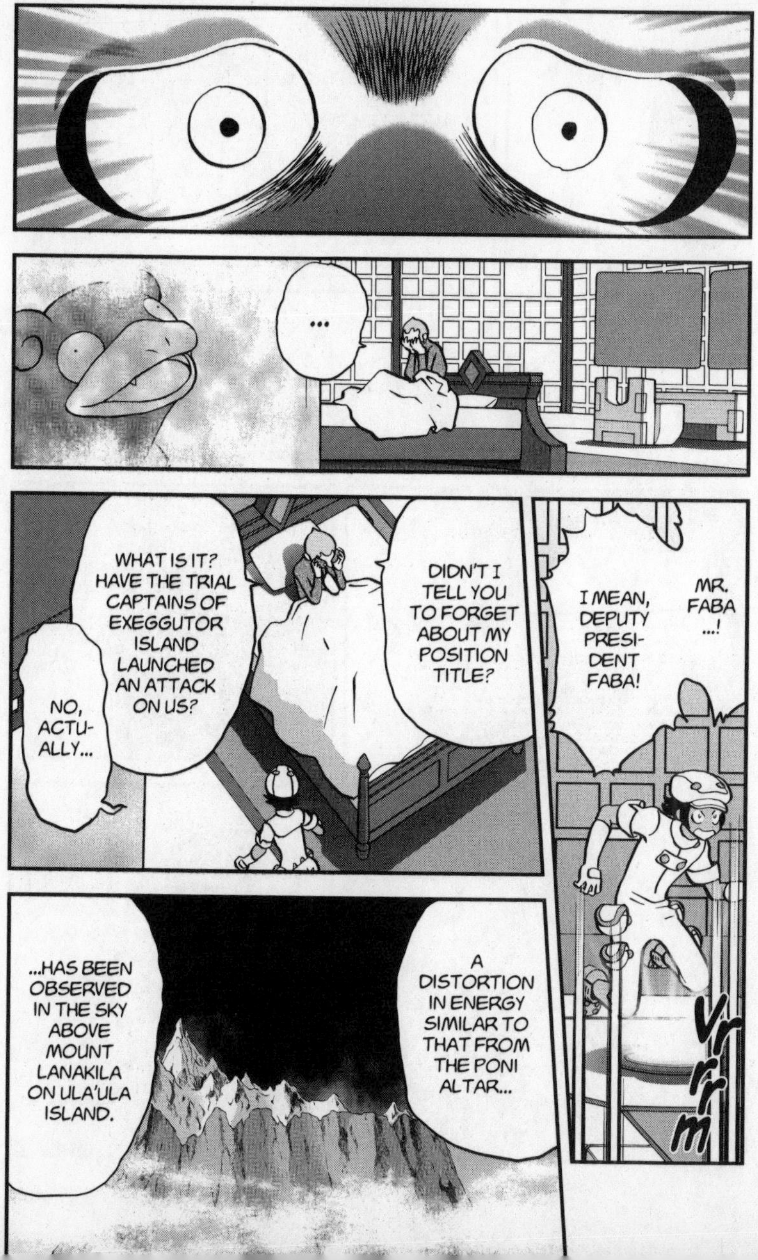
...
MR. FABA ...!
I MEAN, DEPUTY PRESI-DENT FABA!
Vrrrm
DIDN'T I TELL YOU TO FORGET ABOUT MY POSITION TITLE?
WHAT IS IT? HAVE THE TRIAL CAPTAINS OF EXEGGUTOR ISLAND LAUNCHED AN ATTACK ON US?
NO, ACTU-ALLY...
A DISTORTION IN ENERGY SIMILAR TO THAT FROM THE PONI ALTAR...
...HAS BEEN OBSERVED IN THE SKY ABOVE MOUNT LANAKILA ON ULA'ULA ISLAND.

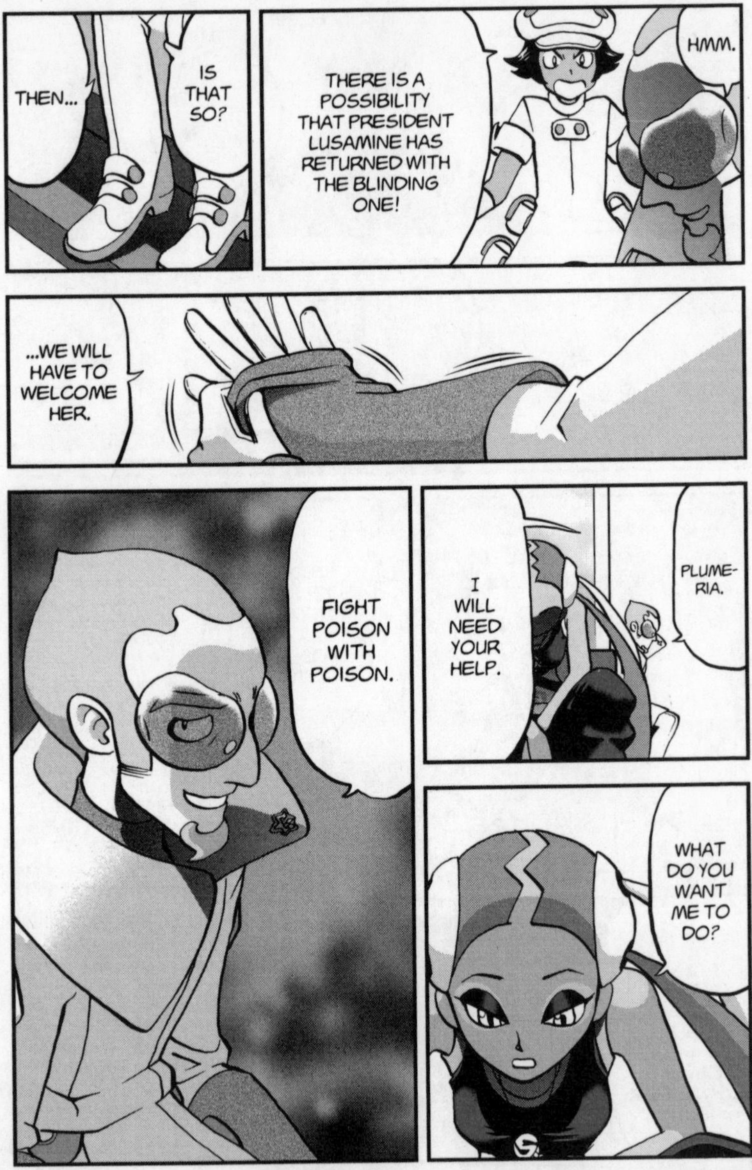
HMM.
THERE IS A POSSIBILITY THAT PRESIDENT LUSAMINE HAS RETURNED WITH THE BLINDING ONE!
IS THAT SO?
THEN...
...WE WILL HAVE TO WELCOME HER.
PLUME-RIA.
I WILL NEED YOUR HELP.
WHAT DO YOU WANT ME TO DO?
FIGHT POISON WITH POISON.

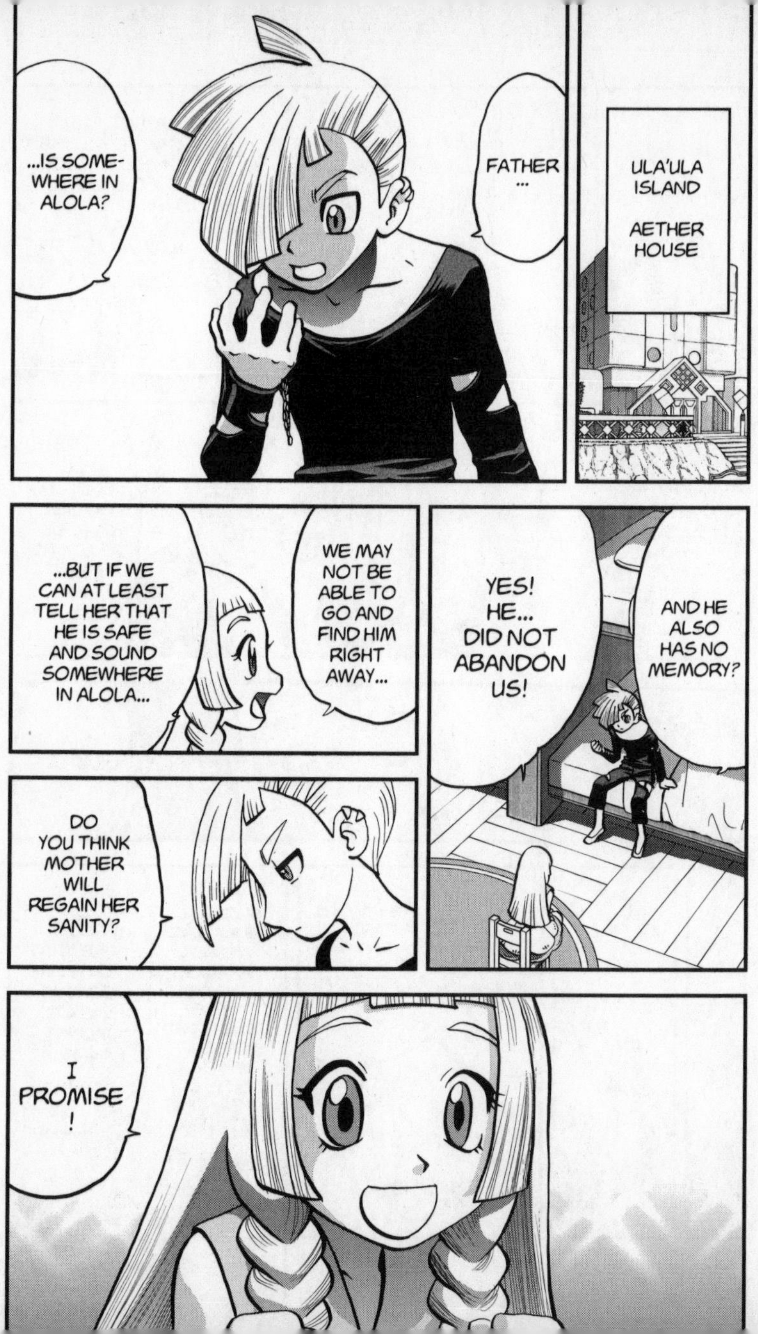
ULA'ULA ISLAND
AETHER HOUSE
FATHER...
...IS SOMEWHERE IN ALOLA?
AND HE ALSO HAS NO MEMORY?
YES! HE... DID NOT ABANDON US!
WE MAY NOT BE ABLE TO GO AND FIND HIM RIGHT AWAY...
...BUT IF WE CAN AT LEAST TELL HER THAT HE IS SAFE AND SOUND SOMEWHERE IN ALOLA...
DO YOU THINK MOTHER WILL REGAIN HER SANITY?
I PROMISE!

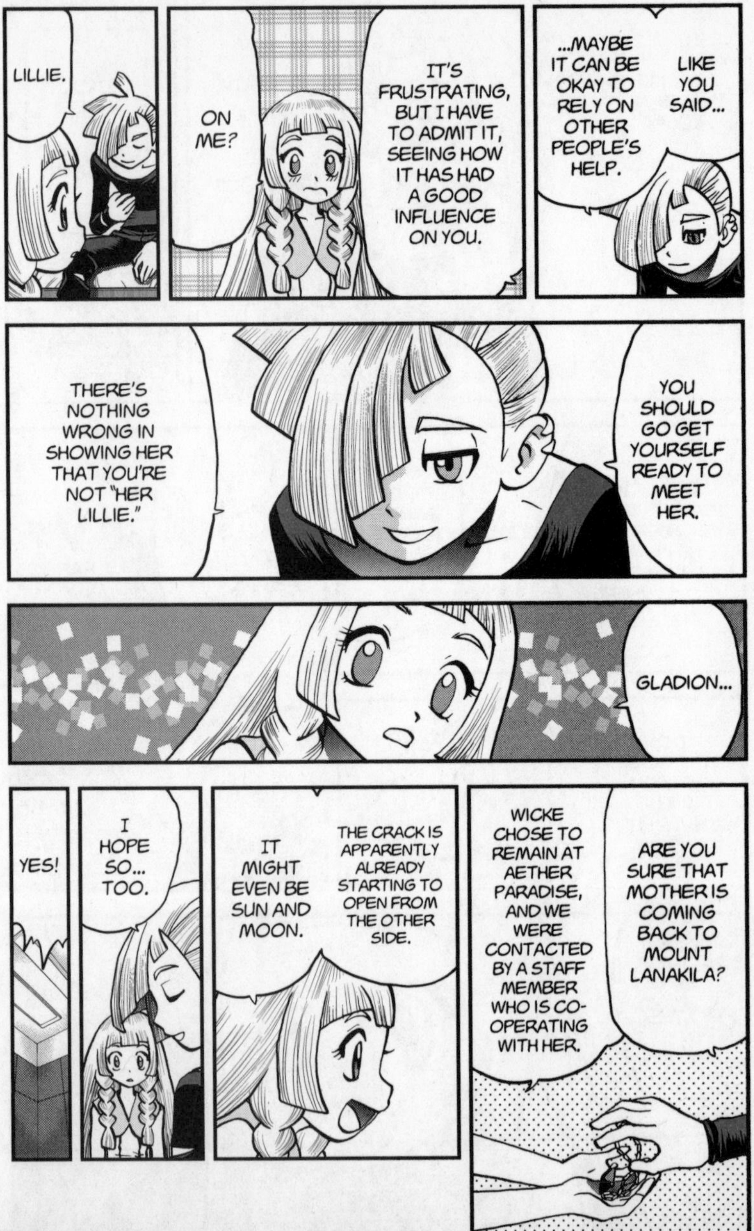
LIKE YOU SAID...
...MAYBE IT CAN BE OKAY TO RELY ON OTHER PEOPLE'S HELP.
IT'S FRUSTRATING, BUT I HAVE TO ADMIT IT, SEEING HOW IT HAS HAD A GOOD INFLUENCE ON YOU.
ON ME?
LILLIE.
YOU SHOULD GO GET YOURSELF READY TO MEET HER.
THERE'S NOTHING WRONG IN SHOWING HER THAT YOU'RE NOT "HER LILLIE."
GLADION...
ARE YOU SURE THAT MOTHER IS COMING BACK TO MOUNT LANAKILA?
WICKE CHOSE TO REMAIN AT AETHER PARADISE, AND WE WERE CONTACTED BY A STAFF MEMBER WHO IS CO-OPERATING WITH HER.
THE CRACK IS APPARENTLY ALREADY STARTING TO OPEN FROM THE OTHER SIDE.
IT MIGHT EVEN BE SUN AND MOON.
I HOPE SO... TOO.
YES!

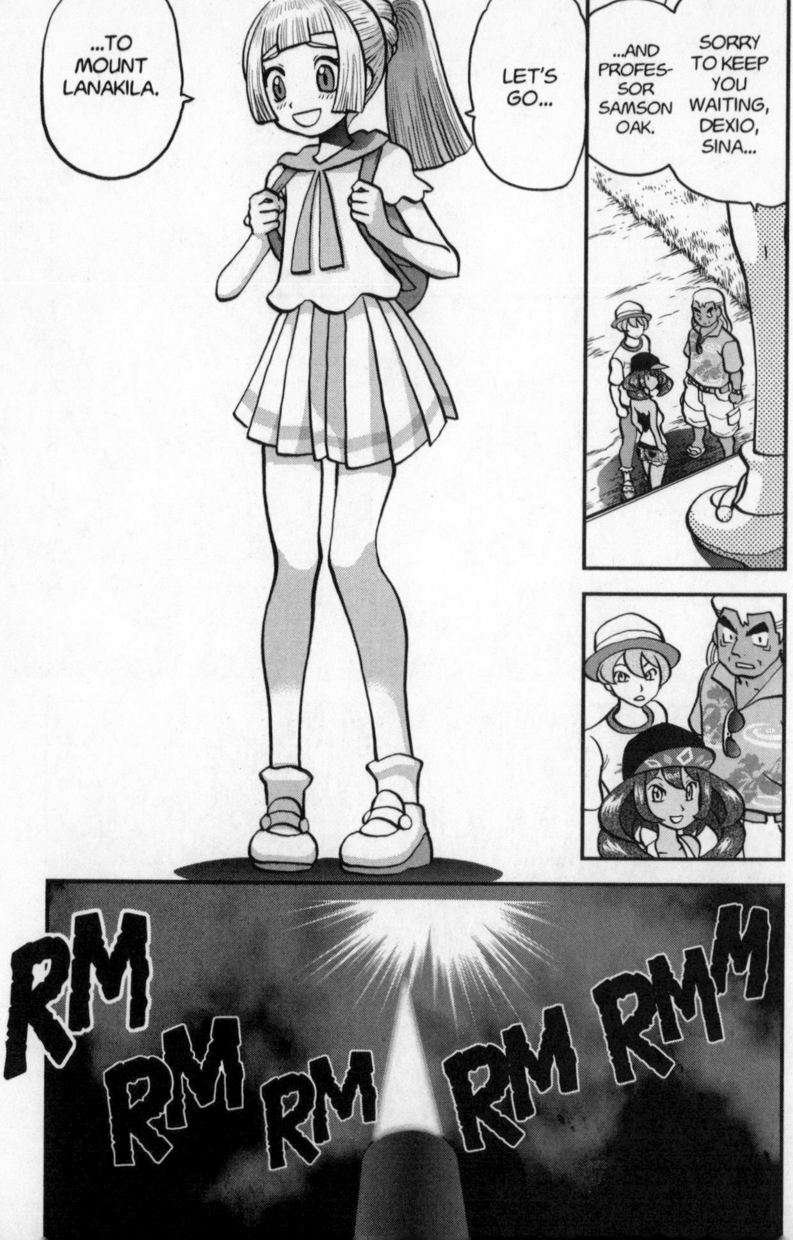

SORRY TO KEEP YOU WAITING, DEXIO, SINA...
...AND PROFES-SOR SAMSON OAK.
LET'S GO...
...TO MOUNT LANAKILA.
RM RM RM RM RM RMM

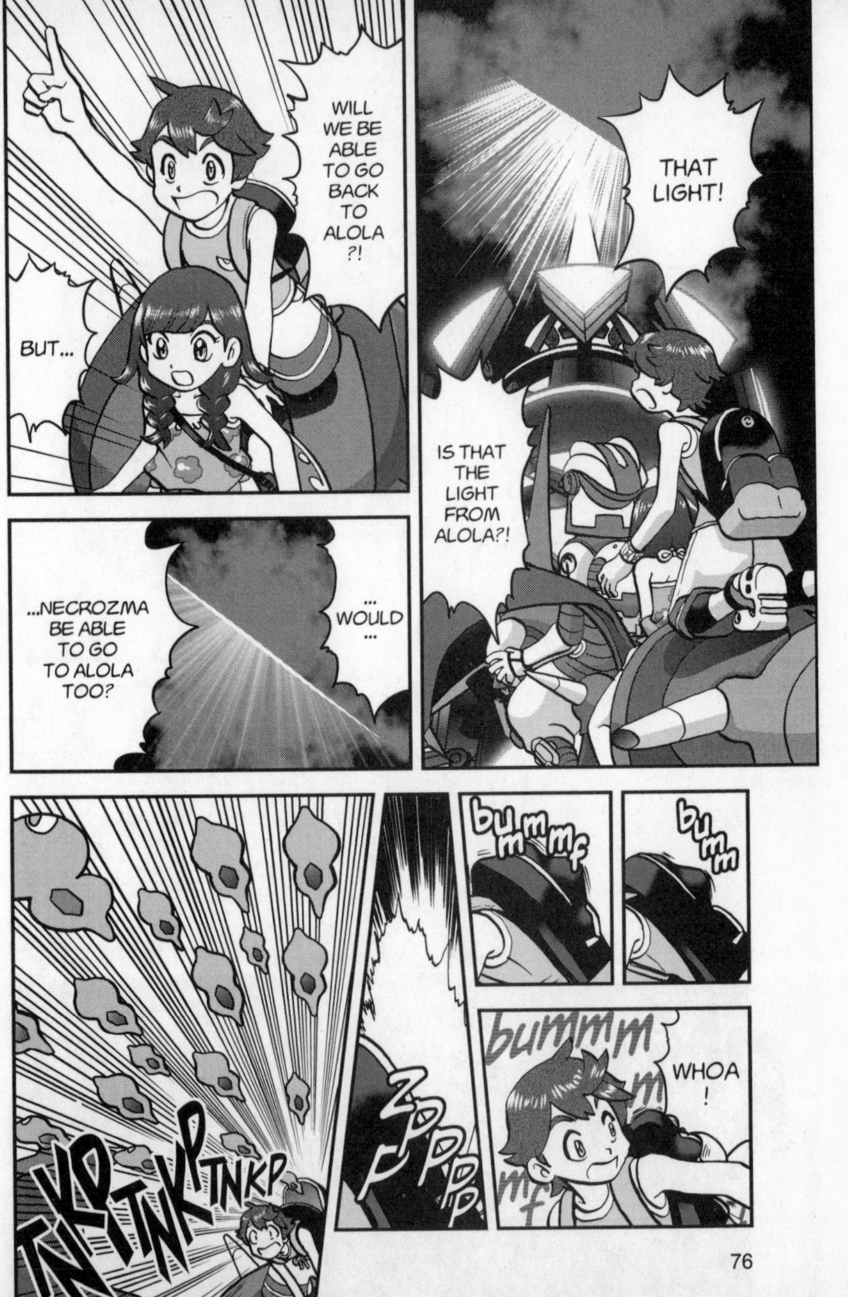
THAT LIGHT!
IS THAT THE LIGHT FROM ALOLA?!
WILL WE BE ABLE TO GO BACK TO ALOLA?!
BUT...
...WOULD...
...NECROZMA BE ABLE TO GO TO ALOLA TOO?
bumm
bummmf
bummm
WHOA!
mf
ZPPPPP
TNKP TNKP TNKP

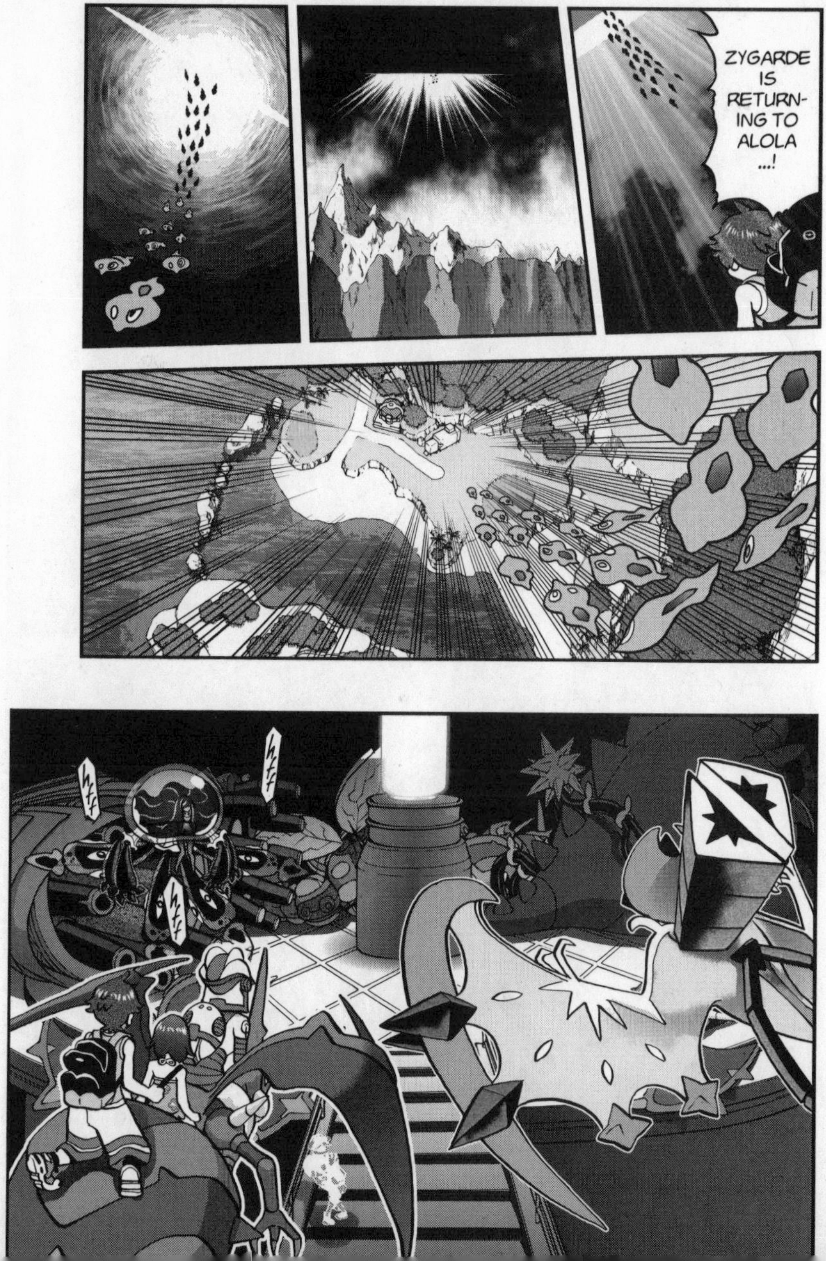
ZYGARDE IS RETURNING TO ALOLA ...!
hff
hff
hff

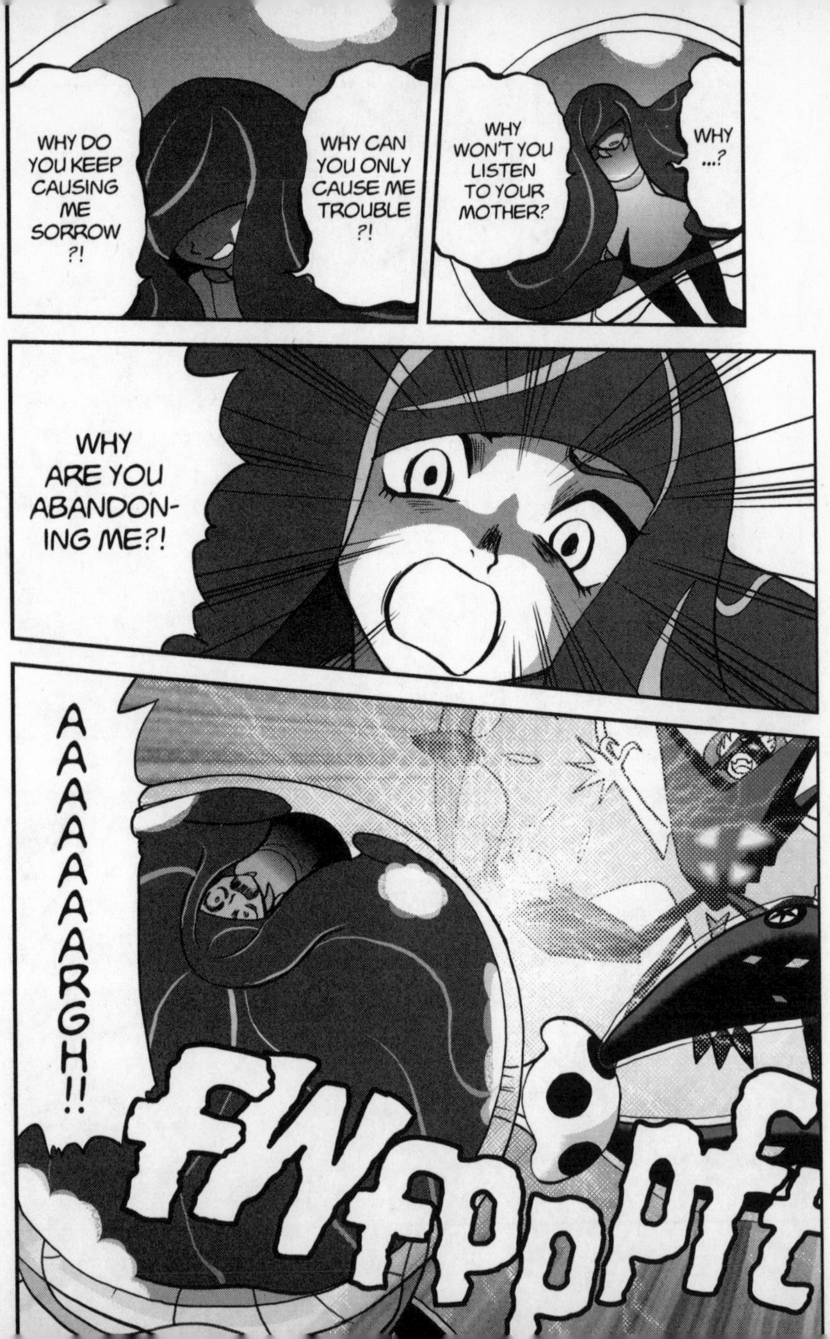
WHY ...?
WHY WON'T YOU LISTEN TO YOUR MOTHER?
WHY CAN YOU ONLY CAUSE ME TROUBLE?!
WHY DO YOU KEEP CAUSING ME SORROW?!
WHY ARE YOU ABANDONING ME?!
AAAAAAARGH!!

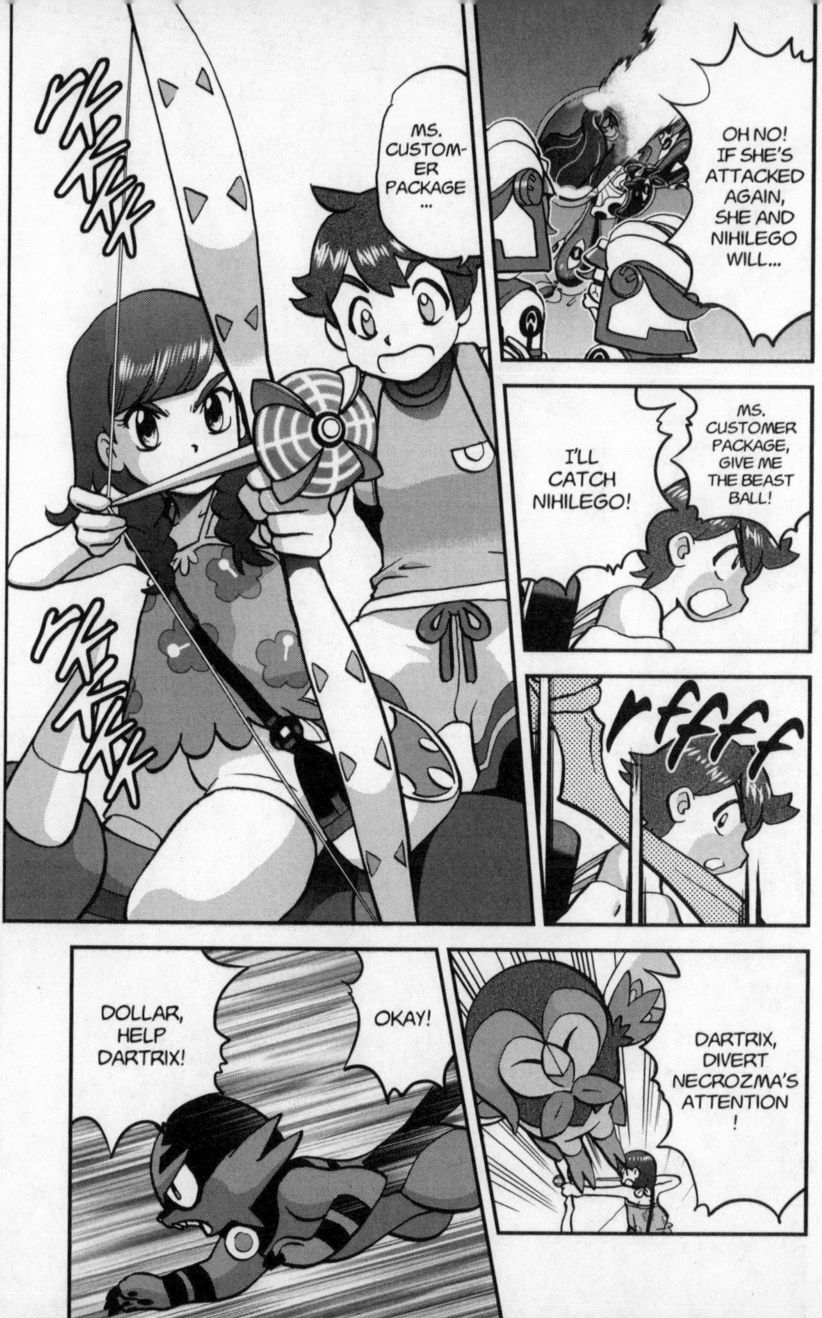
OH NO! IF SHE'S ATTACKED AGAIN, SHE AND NIHILEGO WILL...
MS. CUSTOMER PACKAGE, GIVE ME THE BEAST BALL!
I'LL CATCH NIHILEGO!
rffff
MS. CUSTOM-ER PACKAGE ...
DARTRIX, DIVERT NECROZMA'S ATTENTION!
DOLLAR, HELP DARTRIX!
OKAY!

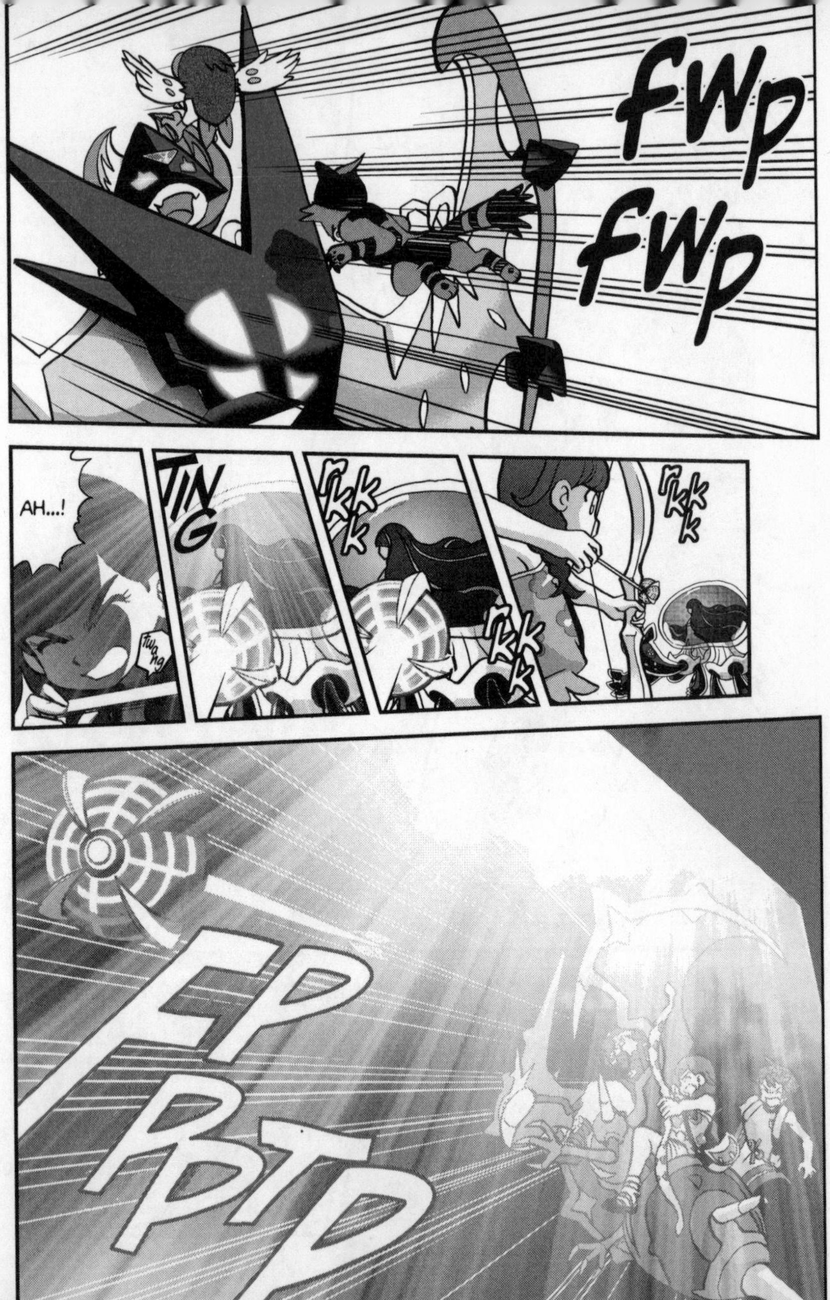
fwp
fwp
rkkk
rkk
rkk
TING
AH...!
twang
FP
FPTP

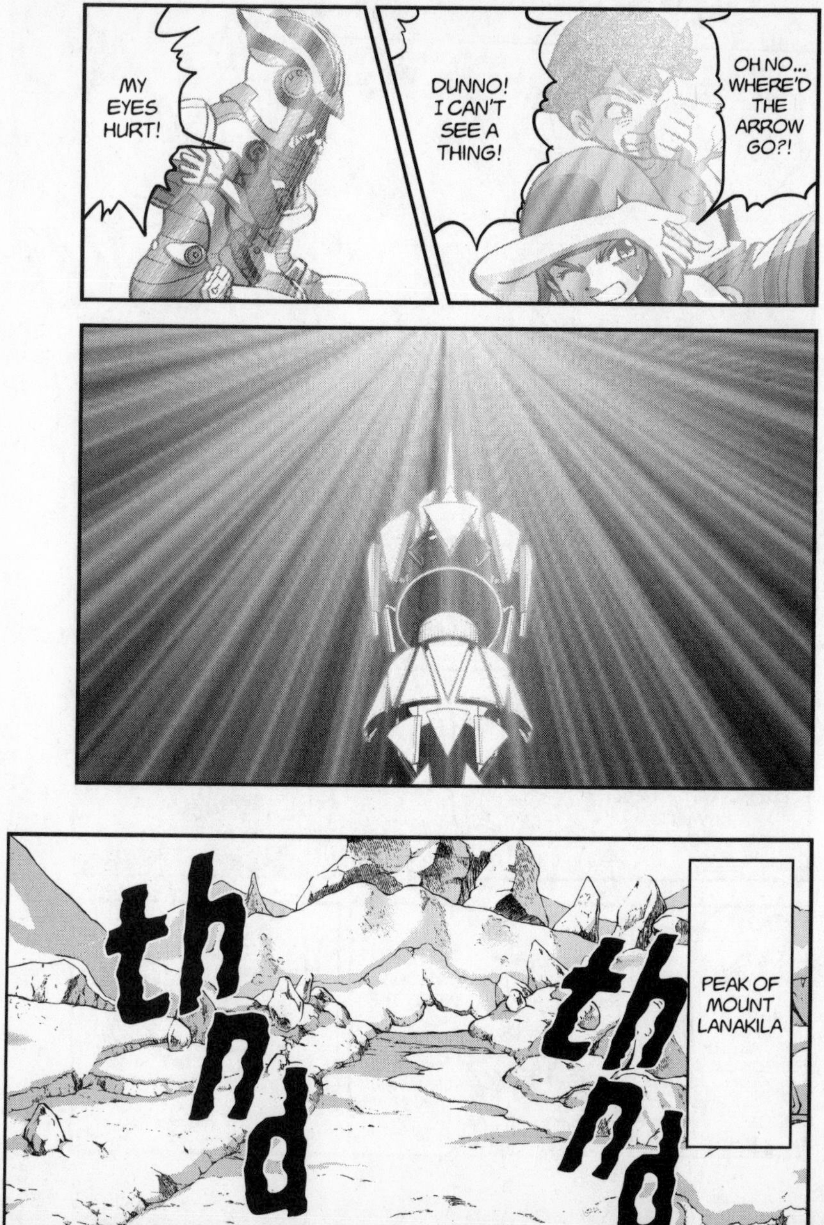
OH NO... WHERE'D THE ARROW GO?!
DUNNO! I CAN'T SEE A THING!
MY EYES HURT!
PEAK OF MOUNT LANAKILA
thnd
thnd

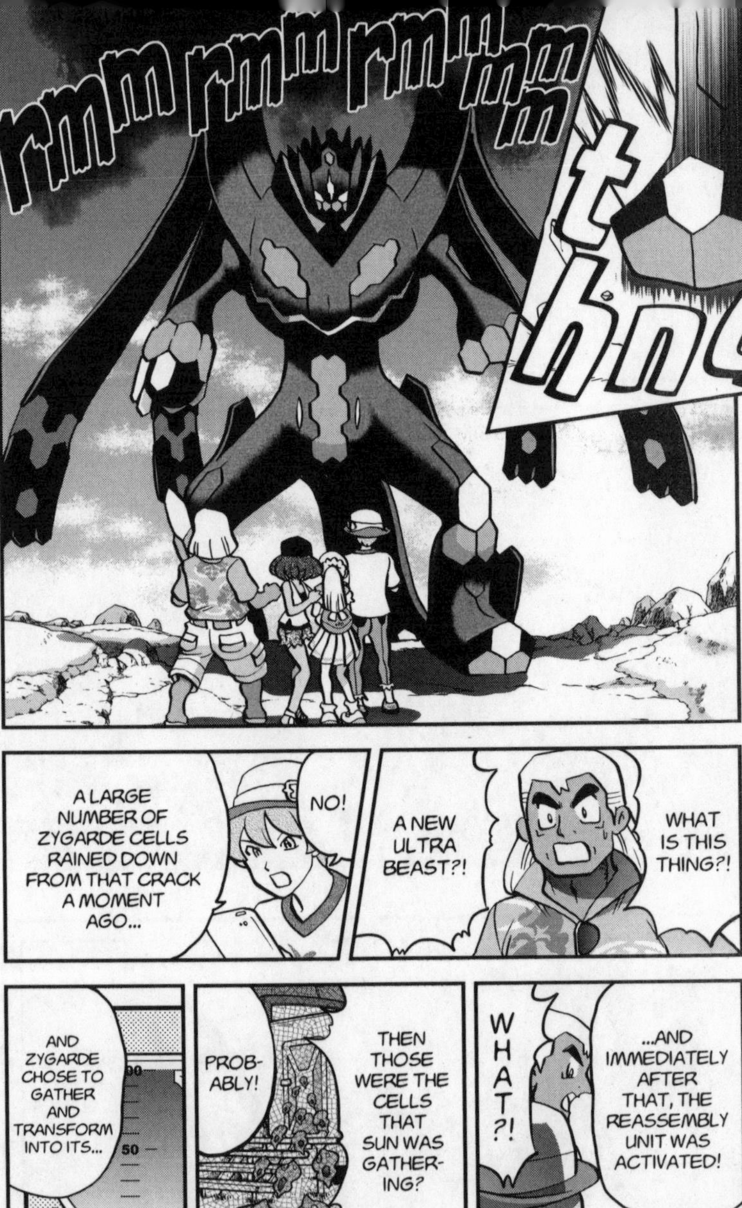
thud
rmmm rmmm rmmm
WHAT IS THIS THING?!
A NEW ULTRA BEAST?!
NO!
A LARGE NUMBER OF ZYGARDE CELLS RAINED DOWN FROM THAT CRACK A MOMENT AGO...
...AND IMMEDIATELY AFTER THAT, THE REASSEMBLY UNIT WAS ACTIVATED!
WHAT?!
THEN THOSE WERE THE CELLS THAT SUN WAS GATHERING?
PROBABLY!
AND ZYGARDE CHOSE TO GATHER AND TRANSFORM INTO ITS...

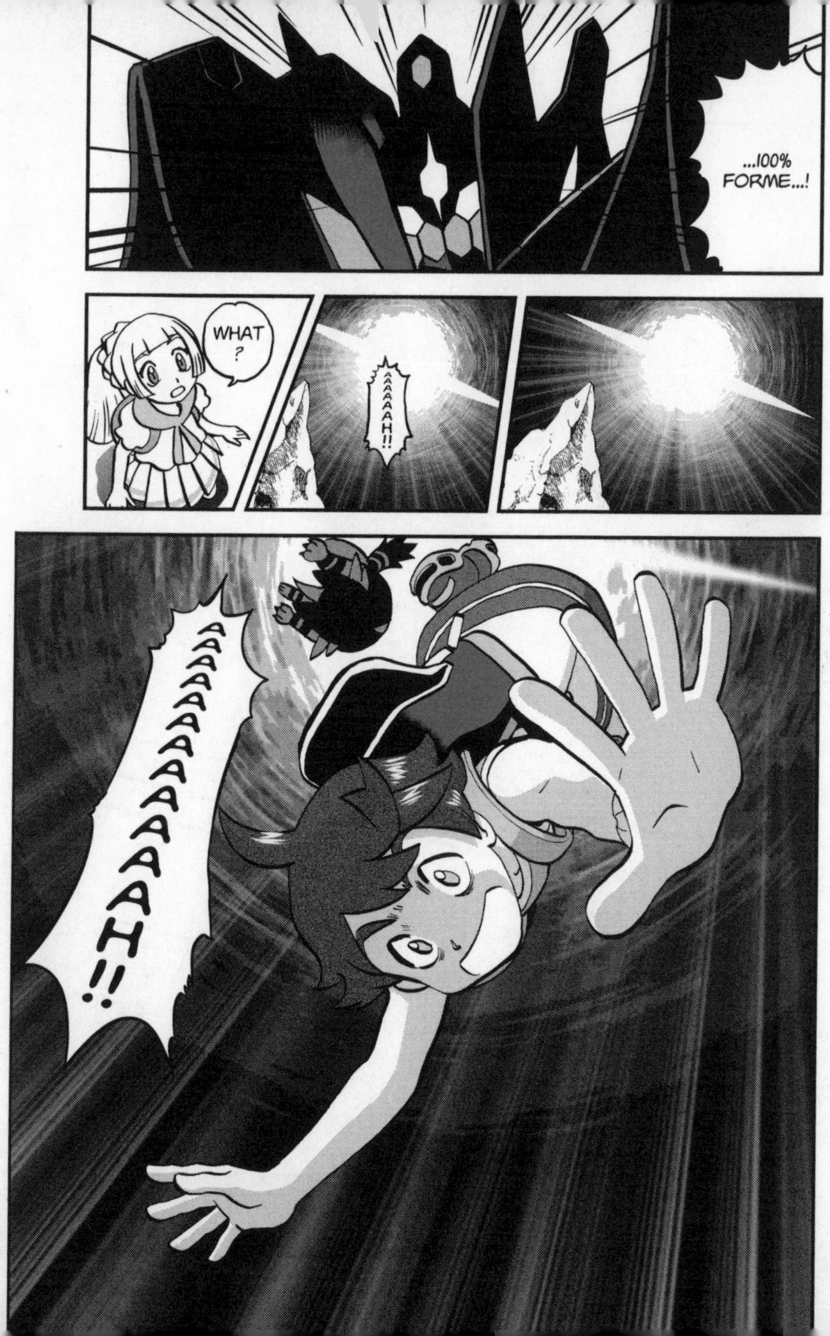
...100% FORME...!
AAAAAAH!!
WHAT ?
AAAAAAAAAAAAH!!

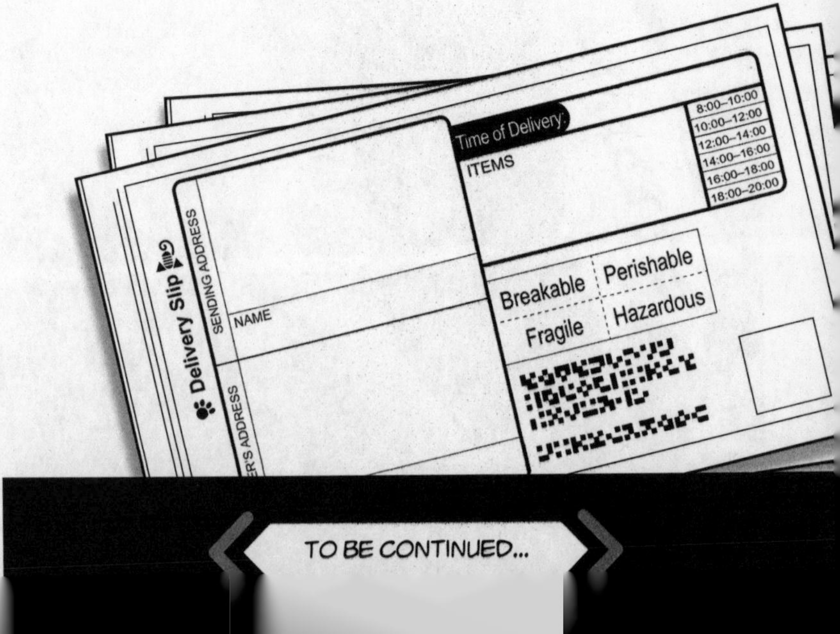
Delivery Slip
SENDING ADDRESS
NAME
Time of Delivery:
ITEMS
8:00–10:00
10:00–12:00
12:00–14:00
14:00–16:00
16:00–18:00
18:00–20:00
Breakable
Perishable
Fragile
Hazardous
TO BE CONTINUED...

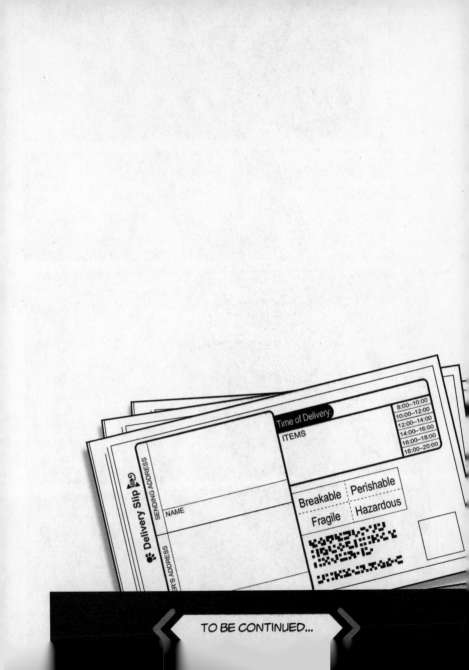

POKÉMON™
SUN & MOON

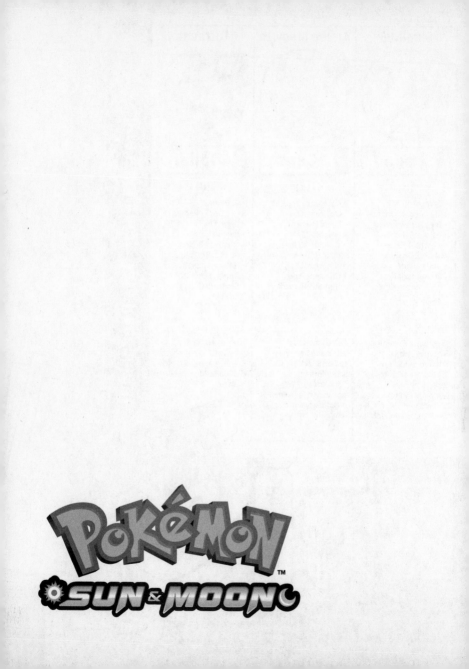

Gather Around!!! Sun's Pokémon Data Revealed!!!

Mimikyu

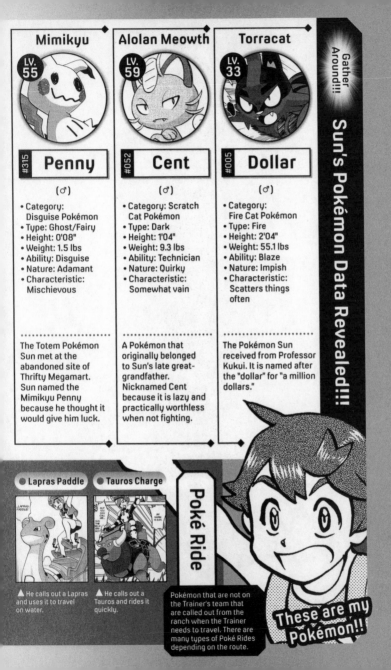

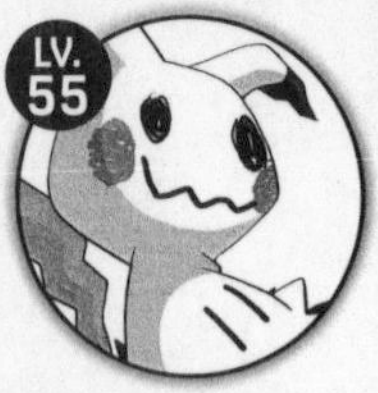
LV.
55

#315 Penny

(♂)

- Category: Disguise Pokémon
- Type: Ghost/Fairy
- Height: 0'08"
- Weight: 1.5 lbs
- Ability: Disguise
- Nature: Adamant
- Characteristic: Mischievous

The Totem Pokémon Sun met at the abandoned site of Thrifty Megamart. Sun named the Mimikyu Penny because he thought it would give him luck.

Alolan Meowth

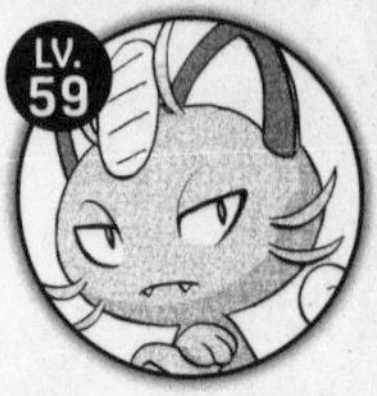
LV.
59

#052 Cent

(♂)

- Category: Scratch Cat Pokémon
- Type: Dark
- Height: 1'04"
- Weight: 9.3 lbs
- Ability: Technician
- Nature: Quirky
- Characteristic: Somewhat vain

A Pokémon that originally belonged to Sun's late great-grandfather. Nicknamed Cent because it is lazy and practically worthless when not fighting.

Torracat

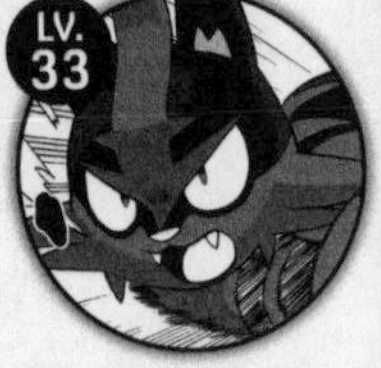
LV.
33

#005 Dollar

(♂)

- Category: Fire Cat Pokémon
- Type: Fire
- Height: 2'04"
- Weight: 55.1 lbs
- Ability: Blaze
- Nature: Impish
- Characteristic: Scatters things often

The Pokémon Sun received from Professor Kukui. It is named after the "dollar" for "a million dollars."

Poké Ride

Pokémon that are not on the Trainer's team that are called out from the ranch when the Trainer needs to travel. There are many types of Poké Rides depending on the route.

Lapras Paddle

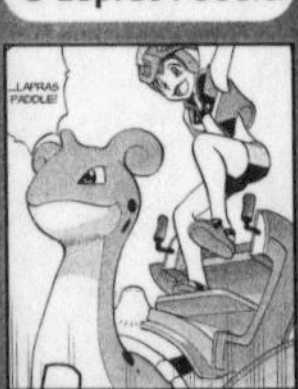
...LAPRAS PADDLE!

▲ He calls out a Lapras and uses it to travel on water.

Tauros Charge

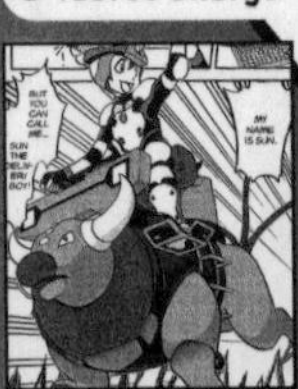
MY NAME IS SUN.
BUT YOU CAN CALL ME...
SUN THE DELIVERY BOY!

▲ He calls out a Tauros and rides it quickly.

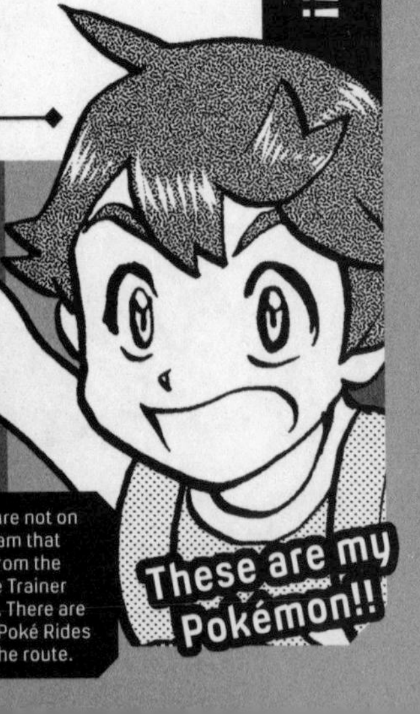
These are my Pokémon!!

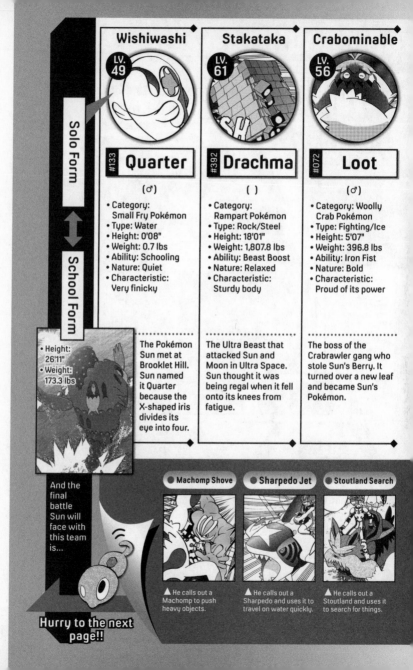

Solo Form

↕

School Form

• Height: 26'11"
• Weight: 173.3 lbs

Wishiwashi

LV. 49

#133 Quarter

(♂)

- Category: Small Fry Pokémon
- Type: Water
- Height: 0'08"
- Weight: 0.7 lbs
- Ability: Schooling
- Nature: Quiet
- Characteristic: Very finicky

The Pokémon Sun met at Brooklet Hill. Sun named it Quarter because the X-shaped iris divides its eye into four.

Stakataka

LV. 61

#392 Drachma

( )

- Category: Rampart Pokémon
- Type: Rock/Steel
- Height: 18'01"
- Weight: 1,807.8 lbs
- Ability: Beast Boost
- Nature: Relaxed
- Characteristic: Sturdy body

The Ultra Beast that attacked Sun and Moon in Ultra Space. Sun thought it was being regal when it fell onto its knees from fatigue.

Crabominable

LV. 56

#072 Loot

(♂)

- Category: Woolly Crab Pokémon
- Type: Fighting/Ice
- Height: 5'07"
- Weight: 396.8 lbs
- Ability: Iron Fist
- Nature: Bold
- Characteristic: Proud of its power

The boss of the Crabrawler gang who stole Sun's Berry. It turned over a new leaf and became Sun's Pokémon.

And the final battle Sun will face with this team is...

Hurry to the next page!!

● Machomp Shove

▲ He calls out a Machomp to push heavy objects.

● Sharpedo Jet

▲ He calls out a Sharpedo and uses it to travel on water quickly.

● Stoutland Search

▲ He calls out a Stoutland and uses it to search for things.

rediction!!!

6 Zygarde

Alola is once again the setting for the battle! These two Pokémon, Necrozma and Zygarde, are the key to the final outcome. Let's analyze how much they've powered up!

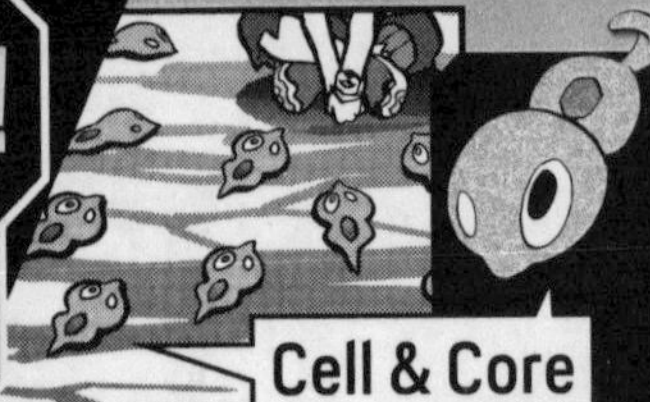

Cell & Core

Small grains which were called "Zygarde Cells" when they were first sighted in the Kalos region. They moved to Alola.

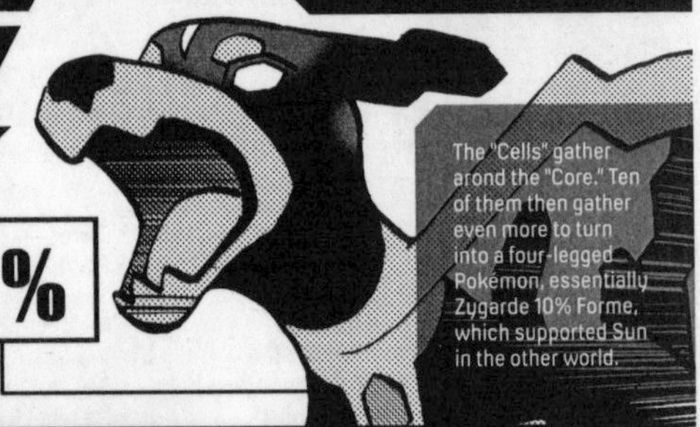

10%

The "Cells" gather arond the "Core." Ten of them then gather even more to turn into a four-legged Pokémon, essentially Zygarde 10% Forme, which supported Sun in the other world.

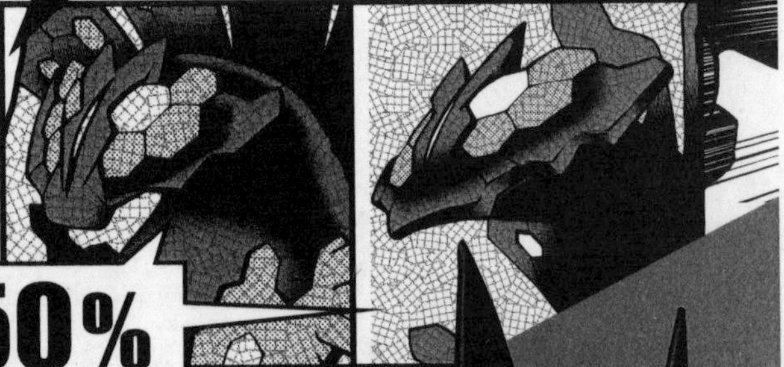

50%

This is Zygarde when 50 of them have assembled together. Let us remind you that they were equally as powerful as Yveltal and Xerneas in this Forme.

DATA

- Category: Order Pokémon
- Type: Dragon/Ground
- Height: 14'09"
- Weight: 1,344.8 lbs
- Ability: Power Construct

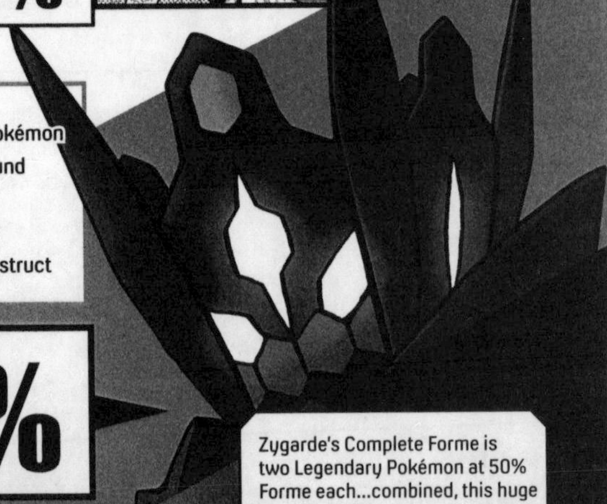

100%

Zygarde's Complete Forme is two Legendary Pokémon at 50% Forme each...combined, this huge humanoid Forme is super strong!

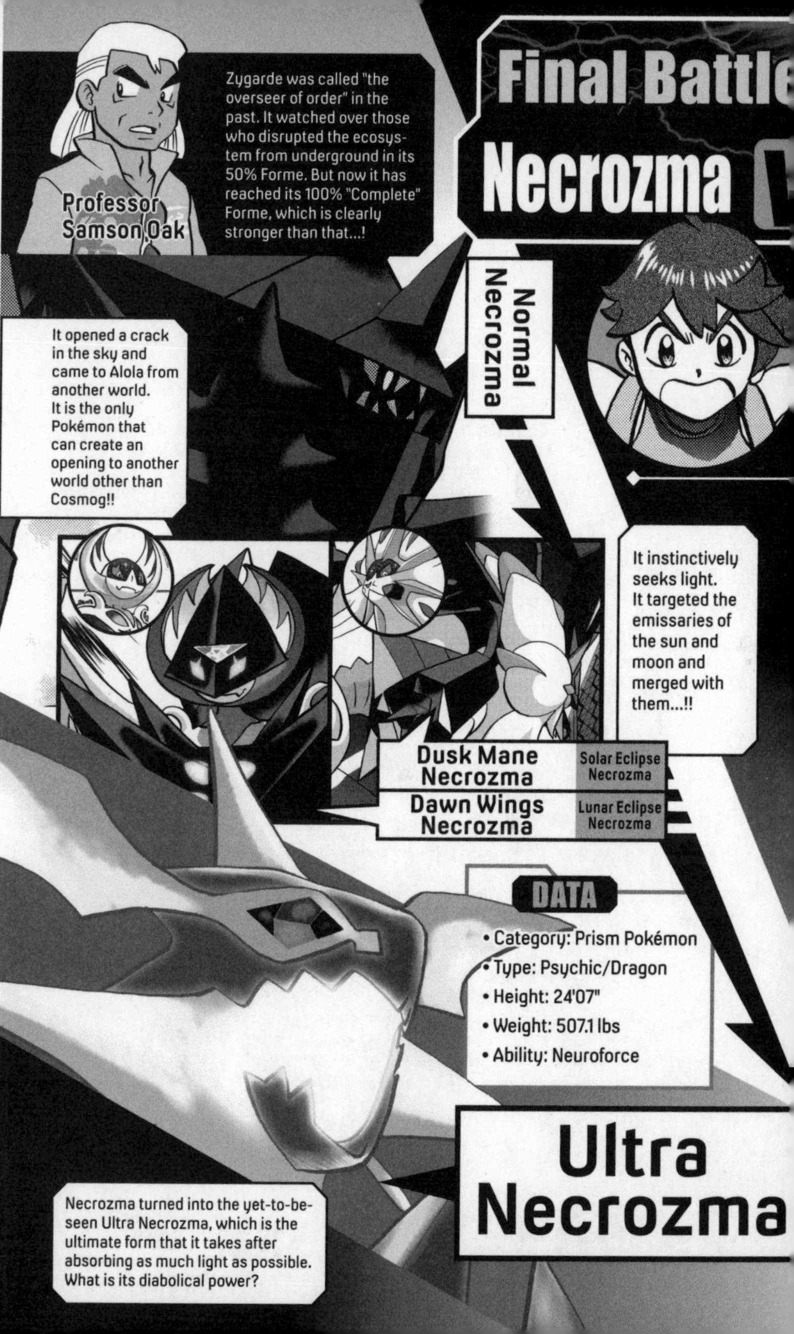

Final Battle
Necrozma
Professor Samson Oak
Zygarde was called "the overseer of order" in the past. It watched over those who disrupted the ecosystem from underground in its 50% Forme. But now it has reached its 100% "Complete" Forme, which is clearly stronger than that...!
Normal Necrozma
It opened a crack in the sky and came to Alola from another world. It is the only Pokémon that can create an opening to another world other than Cosmog!!
It instinctively seeks light. It targeted the emissaries of the sun and moon and merged with them...!!
Dusk Mane Necrozma
Solar Eclipse Necrozma
Dawn Wings Necrozma
Lunar Eclipse Necrozma
DATA
• Category: Prism Pokémon
• Type: Psychic/Dragon
• Height: 24'07"
• Weight: 507.1 lbs
• Ability: Neuroforce
Ultra Necrozma
Necrozma turned into the yet-to-be-seen Ultra Necrozma, which is the ultimate form that it takes after absorbing as much light as possible. What is its diabolical power?

**Pokémon Sun & Moon
Volume 10
VIZ Media Edition**

Story by HIDENORI KUSAKA
Art by SATOSHI YAMAMOTO

©2021 Pokémon.
©1995–2019 Nintendo / Creatures Inc. / GAME FREAK inc.
TM, ®, and character names are trademarks of Nintendo.
POCKET MONSTERS SPECIAL SUN • MOON Vol. 5
by Hidenori KUSAKA, Satoshi YAMAMOTO
© 2017 Hidenori KUSAKA, Satoshi YAMAMOTO
All rights reserved.
Original Japanese edition published by SHOGAKUKAN.
English translation rights in the United States of America, Canada, the United Kingdom,
Ireland, Australia and New Zealand arranged with SHOGAKUKAN.

Original Cover Design—Hiroyuki KAWASOME (grafio)

Translation—Tetsuichiro Miyaki
English Adaptation—Bryant Turnage
Touch-Up & Lettering—Susan Daigle-Leach
Cover Color—Philana Chen
Design—Alice Lewis
Editor—Joel Enos

Printed in the U.S.A.

Published by
VIZ Media, LLC
P.O. Box 77010
San Francisco, CA 94107

10 9 8 7 6 5 4 3 2 1
First printing, May 2021

viz.com

Coming Next Volume

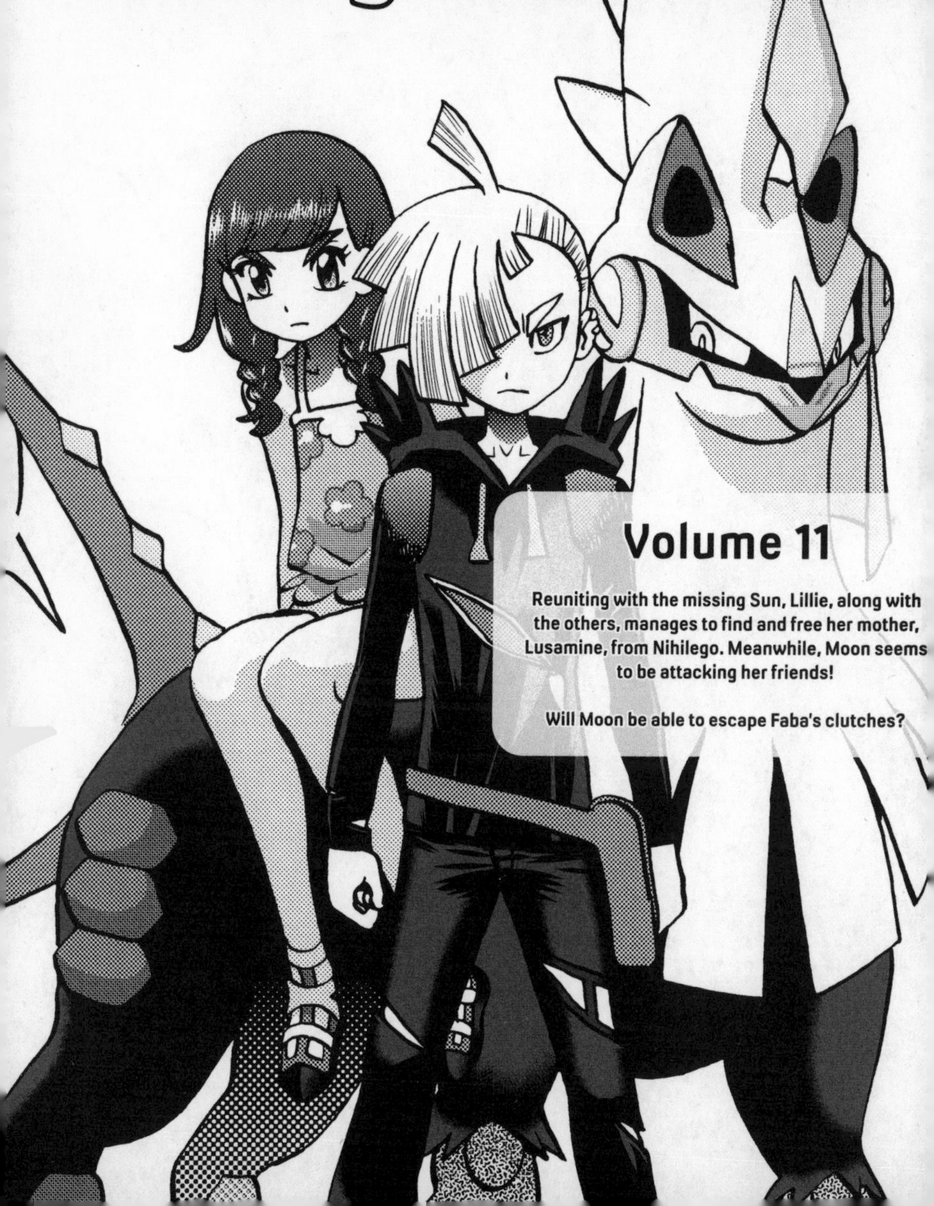

Volume 11

Reuniting with the missing Sun, Lillie, along with the others, manages to find and free her mother, Lusamine, from Nihilego. Meanwhile, Moon seems to be attacking her friends!

Will Moon be able to escape Faba's clutches?

POKÉMON

MEWTWO STRIKES BACK

EVOLUTION

Story and Art by **Machito Gomi**

Original Concept by Satoshi Tajiri
Supervised by Tsunekazu Ishihara
Script by Takeshi Shudo

A manga adventure inspired by the hit Pokémon movie!

Pokémon

Ω RUBY • α SAPPHIRE
OMEGA • ALPHA

Awesome adventures inspired by the best-selling video games!

Picks up where the Pokémon Adventur Ruby & Sapphire saga left off!

STORY BY
HIDENORI KUSAKA

ART BY
SATOSHI YAMAMOTO

POKÉMON ADVENTURES 20TH ANNIVERSARY ILLUSTRATION BOOK

THE ART OF POKéMON ADVENTURES™

STORY AND ART BY
Satoshi Yamamoto

A collection of beautiful full-color art from the artist of the Pokémon Adventures graphic novel series! In addition to illustrations of your favorite Pokémon, this vibrant volume includes exclusive sketches and storyboards, four pull-out posters, and an exclusive manga side story!

viz.com

POKéMON™
SEEK AND FIND

Find your favorite Pokémon in five different full-color activity books! Pick your adventure: will you search for the special Pokémon of Kanto, Johto, or Hoenn? Or will you seek fan favorites like Pikachu or Legendary Pokémon? Each book includes tons of Pokémon-packed seek-and-find illustrations as well as fun facts or creative quizzes about the Pokémon inside.

viz.com

THIS IS THE END OF THIS GRAPHIC NOVEL!

To properly enjoy this VIZ Media graphic novel, please turn it around and begin reading from right to left.

This book has been printed in the original Japanese format in order to preserve the orientation of the original artwork. Have fun with it!

4
3
2
1
2
1
8
7
6
5
4
3
9
5
142

Follow the action this way.

READ THIS WAY!

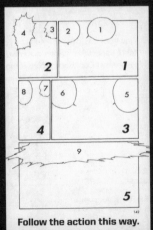